CIRCUMSTANCES
Unraveled

A Circumstances Novel

JEAN KELSO

CIRCUMSTANCES UNRAVELED

Editing, Interior Design, & Formatting by:
Fancy Pants Book Formatting
Cover by Just Write Creations
ISBN: 978-0-9951929-7-3

JEAN KELSO

DEDICATION

For Shannon,
Thank you for always pushing me, supporting me and having faith in me. I love you, chick.

CIRCUMSTANCES UNRAVELED

DISCLAIMER

CIRCUMSTANCES UNRAVELED

ACKNOWLEDGMENTS

Where to start…

I want to thank everyone who wanted more from these characters. I pray I did them justice for you. I love this story, and I hope you do too.

Thank you to my beta group, Shannon, Amy, Dawn, Brandy, and Angi. A special thank you to Julie Solorio for beta reading when the story was finished.

Thank you to my readers for taking the time out of your day to read this book. Without you, there would be no one out there to enjoy my story.

Thank you to my family and friends for always being by my side. I love you.

To Casey Harvell. You are da bomb girl. Editing and formatting. THANK YOU! Your business Fancy Pants Formatting is amazing! She helps me with so much, love you, girl!

To JM Walker at Just Write Creations. You created an amazing cover. Thank you so much.

To any and all blogs who help spread word of my stories, I thank you. You all work so hard and I appreciate you.

Thank you, thank you, thank you to everyone and anyone out there who supports my writing and stories. Your love and support means so much to me!

CIRCUMSTANCES UNRAVELED

CONTENTS

PROLOGUE
Mel

The judge looks like he's already made his decision. His eyes are glazed-over and he stares at nothing in particular. I'm the only witness they have to take the stand. Beads of sweat glisten on my forehead. I can feel eyes glaring at me as the tiny hairs on the back of neck stand on end, causing a chill to run down my spine.

My name (Mel Snow) is called, so I slowly get up out of my seat behind the counsel and follow the bailiff to take the stand. Before I sit, I'm sworn in. "Do you solemnly swear to tell the truth, the whole truth, and nothing but the truth, so help you god?" The bailiff asks as he holds the bible between us.

I place my right hand on top of the book and my body trembles. Looking around the court room, my breathing begins to slow until my eyes land on theirs. Riley Daniels and Matt Booker. The two men I'm testifying against on Belle's behalf. Another chill runs down my spine. The chill I had moments ago was nothing compared to the one that runs through my entire body now.

I didn't want Belle having to go through any more stress of lawyers and courtrooms than she already had with her case against Mike—her main rapist—so when the prosecutor asked if I'd stand up as the sole witness against Mike's accomplices, I couldn't say no.

Turning my eyes back to the bailiff I swallow deeply. "I do." I say as clearly as I can.

The bailiff looks to the judge and back to me. He nods as he speaks. "You may have a seat."

I sit in the witness chair and anxiously await questioning to begin.

Being the only witness for the case, I hope I'm enough help for the prosecution. I only saw the two men come from the room where I found Belle partially naked, abused with bruises forming and in distress. But then again, I suppose any little bit of information, helps.

Questions are being yelled and argued by the prosecutor and defense. Some are basic, but some are pretty intense. The lawyers even argue among themselves. I'm not sure if they want me to answer those ones or not. But when it's time, I take hold of all the courage I can manage and answer to the best of my knowledge. After my testimony, it doesn't take long for the proceedings to finish up and a guilty verdict is handed to both men.

A weight feels as though it has been lifted off my shoulders when the judge reveals the verdict. Now all three men will be behind bars for the rape of my friend. I take a deep breath and look back at Riley and Matt one last time. The looks that flash back manage to thrust further weight on my shoulders. Something doesn't seem right. Riley is smirking as Matt points to me shaking his head. His finger curls in with the rest to make a fist. A small punching motion is made to his other hand, then he smirks.

Did he or the pair of them just threaten me?

I quickly look around the court room, but nobody seems to have noticed their threatening gestures.

Pulling my purse strap over my shoulder, I try to push the incident aside. I stand and proceed to leave the court room. It's time to move on from all this. I need to get back to Belle since she doesn't know I'm here today. No more stress for my girl.

Time to take control.

CIRCUMSTANCES UNRAVELED

CHAPTER ONE
Mel

Eight Years Later

I can't believe I've kept this secret for so long. Belle deserves to know that I stood up in court on her behalf. She also deserves to know about my past, but with everything that just happened I don't want to stress her out anymore. I suppose it can be a secret for a little while longer. I just hope she doesn't ask questions about that text.

It's been two weeks since she got the text message, *The boys are back in town*, the one that was intended for me. Mike must have been in contact with his friends, Riley and Matt all along. Things didn't work out in Mike's favor and he's (of course) back behind bars. But would Riley and Matt be stupid enough to try something again?

I sit in the café drinking my morning caffeine fix pondering these thoughts when out of the corner of my eye I see Jack walk in. I don't think he sees me which is okay, I still get a little shy when he's around. He's too good looking and intimidating for his own good. I felt a strange, comfortable connection when he was near before, but he didn't seem to show an interest when I last saw him. The case ended with Belle and Gabe. Jack seems to have disappeared into the wind.

I'm so easily forgotten, Belle thinks I'm this super-hot chick that can get whoever I want, but she's wrong. I'm good at hiding things from her—good at playing it up to make things look better than they do—because I want Belle to be happy. I put on a good front, but when I'm alone, I truly am alone.

If she only knew.

Staring into my cappuccino, dazed in my own world, I don't hear him approach.

"Mel, is that you?" A husky voice asks.

I'll never forget that voice. I close my eyes tight as I faze back into reality. Turning my head to look to him I smile. "Jack." The sexy man of my dreams, wet and dry. Jack.

"I thought that was you." He looks around the café and back to me. "You're all alone. Where's Belle today? I thought you two were a pair?" He chuckles.

I laugh lightly and smile. "She's home with Gabe today. I'm heading into work to catch up on some paperwork this morning." I pick up my mug and sip my drink quietly. I sort of want to ask him to sit with me, but the shy part of me screams no. It's so hard to put myself out there, to be forward with a stranger who's out of my league. Now a co-worker, someone I've known a while…that's different. They're on the same level as me. Jack. He's on a whole other plane. I'd never meet his standards.

Jack put his hand in the pocket of his blue jeans and shifts his boot covered feet. "Well, I was just grabbing a coffee to go. Just wanted to say hello. I'm staying in the city longer, planting some roots. Maybe we'll bump into each other again." He smiles and nods.

"Sounds good to me. Take care, Jack."

He walks away.

Finishing my drink, I pick up my purse from the table and head toward the door. I told my supervisor I'd be in by eight to finish up the reports from the evening before and I don't want to be late.

The hospital is just down the street from the café. The early morning is busy as usual with traffic in grid lock from corner to corner and people rushing along the sidewalk. I bustle my way toward the corner when the hair on the back of my neck stands up. Stopping in my tracks I look around, someone bumps into me and I apologize for my immediate stop. The person just keeps walking. The eerie feeling doesn't subside, even though nothing out of the ordinary appears. I look around again to see what could be causing the odd reaction...but still nothing, so I keep moving.

The light at the street corner is red, so I stop with the group of people there. Many of them on cell phones chattering away. Me? My thoughts are focused on the paper work I need to get done.

Suddenly a hand is on my hip and then my other. I tense. A hard body of sorts leans into me. "Act normal and follow my lead if you want to live." The deep harsh voice blowing hot on my neck tells me. The voice is oddly familiar. I believe I've heard it before, but I'm not sure from where. My instincts tell me to run—but I also want to live, so I think I'll do as the voice tells me. Instinctively, I want to reach into my purse for my phone, but I don't want to risk the man catching me doing it. Why are people so easily preoccupied, never paying attention to their surroundings? Doesn't anyone notice what's going on? Fuck my life.

I nod my head, my dark locks shifting as I do. "Okay." I whisper softly, praying he heard.

I'm pushed forward when the light turns green and directed across the street but not in the direction of the hospital. A shiver runs up my spine. My mind swims with nervous thoughts. We move toward a dark SUV where a dark figure sits in the driver's seat already. The passenger door opens. "Get in, buckle up and don't say a word." The deep voice tells me. It's then I feel a hard object push into my spine urging me into the vehicle.

My hearts races at what I assume is a gun presses at my back. It's hard to breathe as my chest constricts my rapid heart. I'm not going to refuse him anything at this point. My hands tremble along with my legs and I rush to get into the parked vehicle. I quickly glance at the driver, but I'm not sure if I recognize him or not with the hat and sun glasses he has on. The door beside me shuts and I jump in my seat. The person whose voice I'd been subjected to following commands from gets in the seat behind me and the door shuts.

Fear begins to kick in, my body begins to shake and I try to speak. Just as I open my mouth, something covers it—a hand with a cloth of sorts. I begin to struggle, I can't breathe. Everything begins to fade.

I woke in a small dark, dirty room a few days ago... at least by my count it's been a few days. It could be longer, but I'm not sure. The smell in the air is putrid and makes me feel nauseous. Very little breeze comes in the tiny window that sits far up in the east corner. It's so small, I doubt a child could fit through it. The thought of escaping through it is impossible. The steel bars that cover the puny window don't help, either. With the room being so dark and dank, my mind is fuzzy and seems to play tricks on me. Often I see this as a dream, but when someone enters the small space I realize that it's my reality. So far I've counted three different men, among them my captors Riley Daniels and Matt Booker. It's been a few years since I've seen them, but they haven't changed much. They're older and a bit rougher around the edges, but still the same douchebags I last saw in the courtroom.

The same men who threatened my life.

They've all had a turn at tossing me around from one man to another, pulling my long hair, ripping my now tattered clothes, and laughing cruelly while I try not to cry from pain and embarrassment. Hitting, kicking, yelling at me, shaming me, and warning me for all the disgusting things to come.

The unknown man has an accent. It may be a Spanish variation, but I'm not sure. I've slowly learned some of the words he says, simple words, like girls and numbers. I overheard Matt calling him Mick, and have learned that they plan to sell us. But who the "us" is, I don't know. So far, I haven't seen anyone but the three men.

I'm in shock at being here, but also shocked to see that Matt and Riley went in this direction, in the twisted life of crime. I mean yeah, they fucked up in college—but they could've turned their lives around. I suppose not everyone takes that opportunity and just keeps digging that hole deeper.

It's sad really. Matt and Riley are both good looking men. But then again, looks aren't everything. Looks can be deceiving. Very deceiving. Matt, Riley, and Mike are three men who are proof.

I've lost track of time between being treated like an animal and sleep deprivation. The lack of food and water hasn't helped me, either. My body aches from the many bruises I've received by the hands of Matt and Riley—and a few from Mick. It's like they're trying to train me like a dog…but no matter what they do to me I won't listen, so they hit me, punch me, and even kick me once I'm down. Riley came in once on his own attempting to "train" me. He used more than his hands with his training. He turned me into a rape victim. Even with that, I'm not ready to give up. Jack needs time to find me. Jack…why didn't I just jump him when I had the chance? My mind's busy while the men work me over. I have to keep a focus on something worth living for. Jack is my reason. Belle is my reason.

They must think I'm sleeping. I overhear Matt discussing another woman. I know it's him by his deep voice. He's the one who nabbed me on the street. Plus, he tends to slur dirty names at me while he beats me. He says something about possibly being followed when they took her, so the warehouse could be under suspicion and that they'd have to move base soon. That must mean that we won't be here much longer. That they're moving me to a new place. That means I don't have long to try and figure out how to get away. I'm not a very strong woman, physically. But I *will* be as strong as I need to be. I *will* fight for my life and there is no way I'm being sold for sex or anything else. I haven't lived to the age of thirty without fighting my demons and praying for angels daily just to give it all up now.

I take a deep breath thinking of any possible scenario where I can get out of this alive. Not many are jumping to me at this point, but like I said I'm not giving up yet. I just told you I had reasons to live, right? I just wish Jack was here. It'd make things so much easier.

If you think about it, if Belle notices I'm missing she'll be on Gabe to find me. I'm her sister. Well, not technically, but close enough…and if Gabe is searching he'll damn well get Jack involved. Jack has connections with the FBI and CSIS (Canadian Security Intelligence Service.) Once he gets working on a case, he doesn't stop until the case is done.

Jack will find me.

I know he will.

I listen to all that I can, tucking all the info I gather into my memory bank. Every little bit of information will help in the long run. I lie quiet and still until someone approaches. I'm not sure who it is, but by the smell they need a shower. The odor is rancid, worse than the smell of this room and vomit is on the rise. I take shallow breaths to prevent the bile from coming up. As I release another breath, I can feel the burn of it my throat.

There's no privacy whatsoever in this God forsaken room. I can smell (and almost taste) anything that comes close. Right about now, I can feel the closeness of a body standing beside the bed I lay on. Heavy breathing blows over me. I clench my eyes tight and pray that whoever is there doesn't try getting frisky with me. I know I can fight back, but with the smell, I'm not sure if I can hold back the vomit for too much longer.

"Such a pretty little thing you are." Mick whispers with his thick accent. It's because of it that I can tell who speaks to me.

A hand grazes my forehead and pulls my hair out of my face. It takes everything in me to stay relaxed and not react. I want to hold my breath, but I know it will only make my nausea worse, so I take slow steady breaths.

"I can do so many wicked things with a woman like you." Mick whispers once more, then my hair is gripped and yanked back.

My head pulls back hard, my eyes open and I cry out. "Ahh…"

I hear running feet. "Let her go, Mick. Now's not the time." Riley yells out.

My hair is released as Mick spits on me. He looks to Riley, "You had her. I want her." He glares back down at me. "Stupid slut. I'll get mine."

Mick gets up and leaves the room. I look around to make sure I'm safe for the moment and curl back up on the bed.

I'm in for more than I think. Now's not the time? Does that mean there will be a time? I really don't like the sounds of that.

I take a deep breath and try to relax. I need to think this through.

How do I get out of this hell hole and survive?

CIRCUMSTANCES UNRAVELED

CHAPTER TWO
Jack

I can't believe I just walked away from that woman again. Opportunity only knocks so many times. It's knocked once when we met at Belle's and it's knocking now. *What am I thinking? Mel turns my crank in more ways than one—such a vulnerable woman ripe for the picking...if I could only get her to see me, the real me.*

I'm not a bad guy.
Really, I'm not.

After leaving the café this morning something felt off. Everything inside me told me to go back and get the girl, but I didn't. I only use my gut when it comes to work and I had work to do. It's always about work. When will I learn to let things go and make some time for myself? Gabe has always nagged on me about that, and especially now that he has his woman, he wants to see me happy too.

I'm not the perfect man, I know that. I've made many mistakes and I'm sure I'll make more. The question is; will Mel—the sweet, sexy, spit fire that she is—tolerate the depths of my errors as they come? My gut says yes, but I don't really know her.

Shutting my laptop, I reach down into the cooler and grab a beer. I know it's only two in the afternoon, but I can't seem to shake this nagging feeling that something's wrong.

Mel was going to work she said. Belle and Gabe are together and no phone calls have come through, so what could be wrong?

I crack open the beer and take a swig. The cold refreshing drink soothes my dry throat. Sitting back in my chair I cross my legs at the ankles and close my eyes. The vision of Mel dances through my mind. The way she looked when I first met her and that mouth of hers. She sure pissed me off with the way she talked to me at first, but I could tell she was playing around, trying to get a feel for me.

Working with the police, the Canadian Government, and the feds over the years I've learned a few things. I know that the way Mel was talking is a defense mechanism. She hides her true self or at least a secret of sorts. She's a shy one under all that fire she spits. But even though she's hiding, she can't hide everything. Like her looks—those gorgeous blue eyes, her long black hair, and her sleek body. I get hard just thinking about her. *Damn, maybe I just need to get laid.*

I shake my head to clear my thoughts, sitting forward and setting my drink on the table. Just then my phone rings. Picking it up, I see it's Gabe calling.

"What's up Gabe?" I ask.

"Hey, man. Have you heard from Mel recently?" Gabe inquired.

"I actually saw her this morning. She was heading into work, why?" My interest is peeked.

A breath blows out on the other end of the line. "She never showed up at work. Belle's freaking out. Mel isn't answering her cell or home phone, either." Gabe says.

She didn't show up for work? Well, fuck me. There's my reason for feeling uneasy. Shit! "Has this ever happened before?" I ask Gabe as I sit up in my seat.

"Nah, man—never. Belle mentioned that she got a weird text a few weeks ago. She didn't understand what it meant or who it was from, but Mel freaked out about it. It doesn't seem coincidental now, especially since Mel isn't answering her phones." Muffles of Belle yelling comes through the line. "Something's going on and we need to find her Jack. After what Belle went through…" Gabe didn't finish his sentence, he didn't have to.

"Fuck!" I clutch my cell tight. "Alright, I'm on my way over." I hang up and begin to pack up my laptop. The reality of the situation hits me hard and my feelings cut me deep. *If something has happened to my firecracker I'm damn sure going to find out and get her back. And when I do I'm going to break her out of that shell of hers and make her mine. There's something about the woman that I felt connected to from the get go and I shouldn't have let it go. Damn it, I'm not letting go now.*

My bag is packed, keys in hand, out the door I go. Heading to Gabe's with my mind set on finding Mel before something bad can happen. *We don't know where she is, or if anyone even took her, so I need to calm my nerves before I flip my lid.*

It takes me about ten minutes to get to Gabe's. I park in front of the bar and grab my stuff as I proceed to let myself in. "Gabe!" I shout as I march up the stairs.

"Yeah, up here, Jack." Gabe calls back.

I open the foyer door and enter the spacious apartment. Belle sits at the dining table with a tall glass of water. Her leg trembles up and down and she clinks her fingers on the glass. I can see the fear in her eyes. She expects the worse.

I set my bag down by the couch and move to sit at the table. Reaching my hand out I take one of Belle's and give it a squeeze. "Tell me what's going on, Belle." I look right into her fear stricken eyes and wait.

Belle licks her lips before she speaks. "Well, for starters Mel never misses work—and if she does she always calls me to let me know what's going on. Secondly, she always answers her phone—if she's at home, or even if she's at work. When I called the hospital they said she didn't show up." Belle sniffs back some tears that I notice begin to fall down her cheeks.

"Tell me about this text message." I nod toward her cell phone.

Immediately Belle lets go of my hand and grabs the phone from beside her and gives it to me. "I never deleted the message. It's from unknown dated two weeks ago." Belle quickly withdraws back into her chair.

I look at the message. *The boys are back in town.* The first thought that comes to mind is, who the fuck are "the boys"? I look to Belle and back to the phone. Setting it on the table I blow out a breath. It's such a basic message, but all so threatening as well. It could mean so much, yet so little. Looking to Belle again, I ask. "Any idea who this could be from?"

Belle bites her lip and shakes her head. "None."

"Mel confided in me a little while back on something. I'm not sure if that has anything to do with this, but it could." Gabe pipes up.

Belle and I both look to him. "Well, what is it, Gabe?" I ask.

Gabe clears his throat looking unsure of himself. "She told me that she was the witness in court to the other men in Belle's rape case." Belle gasps and I clench my fists.

"She never told me about that. I thought they were just put away along with Mike." Belle whispers. "How stupid can I be? Damn it, Mel."

"I'm sorry I never told you that she told me." Gabe tells her.

Anger boils deep inside of me. *Why can't life just be simple for once? Time to dig into my tech side and see if I can find where the text originated from if possible and to check if there are any cameras by the café. If it was those men, I'll find out somehow.*

"Let's get this started, Gabe." I look to Belle. "We'll find her!" I say to comfort Belle, but inside I'm trying to convince myself that Mel's safe and unharmed. Standing from my chair, I head to my bags

29

to get my computer to start the search for Mel. We have absolutely no leads, but I'm not a man without resources. I'll use what I can and I'll find my woman.

CHAPTER THREE
Mel

Riley comes into the room and escorts me out to an open area full of women. All the women are around my age and younger. There doesn't seem to be anyone older than me here. I feel disgust, embarrassment, and anger. How did these men get away with taking me and all the others? How dare they do the things they do and think that it's okay? I feel like puking from my thoughts, from the pain of the beatings, from just everything.

I start to count the group of us. There are ten of us. We're all filthy and barely clothed. One by one the men begin to blind fold us, tie our hands behind our backs, and lead us out of the room. None of us fight— it's like we know better. If we did, we'd just get smacked in one way or another. I need to wait and pick my moment, timing is everything.

We are put in a truck or van. I'm not a hundred percent sure. I just know it's big enough to hold us all. There are no windows. It's dark and it smells horrible.

Just after the door slams shut and locks, the sobbing begins. Not from me, but the other women. It takes everything in my power to control my emotions. I need to stay strong—if not for me, for them. Some of them look like they just hit puberty for fuck sakes. Someone needs to show them that it's okay to fight back, to not be weak…but then again not everyone has a past like me and can handle some of the crap these guys are dishing out. Sure, I'm shy. I have my reasons, but when it comes to survival? I fight. Now is the time for that fight.

I'm not sure if Riley or the other men in the front of the vehicle can hear or see us, but I want to calm the women. Getting themselves worked up isn't going to help any of us.

"Shhh…ladies calm down, please. Try." I whisper, but it doesn't seem to help any. The women seem to ignore me. I want to help, but I can't help the unwilling. I get as comfortable as I can in an unknown space with my hands tied behind my back while blind folded and wait out the ride.

The ride's a bumpy one and it seems like we drive for hours. We probably do. The doors open suddenly and one by one they begin to call our names. The women whimper this time. The fear of the unknown can't be hidden.

They call me. I do my best to maneuver myself up from the floor of the vehicle. A hand grasps me, pulling me forward, and I stumble.

"There's my girl." The voice I recognize as Matt, growls. "You remember me, don't you? I remember you. I remember that court room, too."

I keep silent and let him direct me. I can feel the edge, thinking I'm going to jump down, when I feel a hand wrap around my hips and hold me tight. He lifts me out and I slide down a muscular body.

Matt, I know his body. He isn't a bad looking guy. Caramel colored skin, light brown eyes, long black hair and muscular body. Not that I can see him now, but I have seen him on occasions while under their 'care'. He has changed for the better looks-wise a little bit since college. In other ways not so much.

"Mmm, I love feeling your body sliding down mine. It makes my dick hard." He squeezes my ass and inhales my scent before setting me down.

It takes everything I have in me not to retch all over him. Matt's a total asshole. He steals and sells women for money. What about that would make me want to like him? Let alone the abuse he has done to me and the other women. I swallow down the bile that has risen in my throat and wait to be led to our new destination.

I can smell the ocean as we stumble along. The shuffling of the women and the other men in front of us is loud against the hard ground. No idea to where we are, I hope it's better than the last. I hear a creaking noise as I assume a door opens and Matt shoves me inside. I trip up a stair that I'm not aware is there and fall to my knees. I wince in pain as it shoots up my legs. I'm lifted by strong arms and pushed forward again.

"Keep going." Matt grumbles.

How such a handsome man can be such a cruel creature, I'll never know. I keep moving forward until someone pulls me in another direction and leads me to sit on what I presume to be a bed. They remove the blindfold and release my hands. I blink a few times as the light is bright after being in the dark for so long and take in my surroundings.

The room is different than the last. It's larger. There are actual clear windows allowing sunlight in, but they are high up on the walls where we're unable to reach—and of course there are bars on them. There are beds laid out (five in total) and only five of us girls are in the room. The others must be in another room. I watch as Matt removes the ties and blind folds off the other women, then he leaves the room, shutting and locking the door behind him.

I blow out a breath and take in the other women. "Are you all okay?" I ask them.

They all keep their heads down and don't speak to me. I get frustrated with this. Why won't the women answer me?

"What the hell is wrong with you ladies, are you all just giving up?" I ask more forcefully. I move closer to the edge of the bed I'm sitting on. I hate being ignored. I'm not much of a talker unless it's something worth saying, so when I speak, I expect an answer. "Fucking answer me!"

One woman looks up. She looks like she wants to say something, but then bows her head again.

What the fuck? Why would these women bow to them so easily? Are they that weak?

Not wanting to talk to the women anymore, not that they were talking anyways, I curl up on my bed and try to get some sleep. One never knows what tomorrow brings.

I'm startled awake by something rough grazing my leg. Immediately, I roll over in the bed with my eyes open wide to see—and an evil grin upon Matt's face greets me. My heart rate increases and my breath catches.

I kick my leg out, trying to remove his hand with no relief. He grabs a hold of my leg and pulls me down on the bed. No one's going to stop it and the more I fight, the more he'll probably enjoy it. The last time, when Riley did this, I struggled and screamed and he relished every part of it.

"My girl's going to give up some sweet pussy to her Matt." He growls as he continues to pull me down on the bed and toss the blankets aside. He doesn't ask me, it's a statement. Like ownership. Shit!

Looking around quickly to see if anyone else is in the room, I see no one. Where did all the women go?

I'm not letting this happen again. I can't. I won't survive it. "NO!" I shout and swing my arm out at him. I hit him in the face, catching him off guard. I wiggle away, but don't get far. Matt pounces on me and pins my arms down.

"What did you just say?" He slaps me hard across the face. It stings and tears well up in my eyes.

Bucking my body to try and fight him off, thrashing and kicking, I yell. "Get the fuck off of me, you asshole. I said no."

I manage to knock Matt off me and onto the ground. I scramble off the bed and begin to head to the door. I need to escape. I have the door open when I hear a loud bang in the air. A sharp pain hits my shoulder and I scream. "Ahhh…" Tears stream down as pain hits and radiates through my arm just below my shoulder. I start to fall.

Footsteps run in my direction. Then my body slams down on the concrete. My head hits the floor. I'm dizzy—and see spots and blood.

"Wrong move, bitch." A slurry voice tells me right before everything goes black.

My eyes open to Riley and Matt. Arms flailing about and mouths moving. The voices jumble. I try to move, but I can't. My vision is blurry and I lie in something wet.

"Fucking idiot…"

"Kill her…"

"Dump her body..."

"Fuck!"

Jumbled messages, I have no idea what is going on. I try to speak. "Ri.."

The men look at me. Riley marches toward me, fist clenched and slam. Sharp pain and nothing.

CHAPTER FOUR

Jack

I can't fucking believe it's been almost two weeks since she has gone missing. Between me and Gabe we've done everything we can to search the city and put feelers out on her. As if life couldn't suck any more, I finally find the woman I want to try a relationship with and on her way to work one day, she disappears. I haven't seen her since.

I know women go missing every day, but you never think it's going to happen to someone you know.

There are missing person's reports filed by myself and by Belle. There has been no contact made to her work, friends, or myself. Her cellphone was found in a dumpster around the corner from the cafe.

Belle has made contact with all her coworkers about the situation and all the friends they have in common. Not a single person has seen or heard from her. It's like she just disappeared completely.

I thought I saw her a few nights ago at Gabe's bar, but it was just a tourist out for a good time. Gabe had to kick me out because it was ladies' night and I was causing a major disturbance once I realized it wasn't Mel. Between the alcohol and the frustration, I was starting to lose my mind. Now that she's missing, Mel has been on my mind non-stop. I don't know why it takes her being gone for me to notice what's right in front of me, but it does.

Since that night, I haven't stopped looking for her. Every lead the police have gotten has resulted in nothing. They're at a stalemate until new evidence comes in, or a new lead presents itself. Because of this, they put the case on hold. I won't stand for that result at all. Mel's out there somewhere. I'll find her somehow. I have money, I have friends, and the resources—so I hope that if and when I find her she's alive and well. And then I plan to do everything in my power possible to deal with the bastards who took her. I'll do what it takes, legal or not.

I grab a cold beer from the fridge, crack it open, and chug it down. The sensation of the cool fluid sliding down my throat feels amazing. I'm not a big drinker, but a nice cold beer can always help chase away the shitty parts of the day.

I open my eyes and look at the clock. My alarm is going to go off in ten minutes. Day seventeen of Mel missing. I'm about ready to shoot every shady-looking man I find.

Since I hacked the CCTV cameras and found the exact time my firecracker was taken and where from, I've devoted all my time to finding her. The person in the video was well hidden and none of us could make out who the man was with the little detail we had. Believe it or not, the man was smart enough to park out of view—because the make and model of the SUV in the video that Mel was shoved into was non-descript and we couldn't make out the plates. We know there's a second man or woman (we aren't a hundred percent sure which) but the view was just a blur. No new leads have come to light since the videos and Gabe and I have been reaching at straws for anything to guide us.

I was born Catholic, but haven't prayed in years. I've lived on luck, but lady luck hasn't helped these past few weeks. I drop to my knees at the side of my bed, clasp my hands together and bow my head to pray. I close my eyes and I let the lord hear me. I shout to the heavens for my Lord's help, or his guidance to get my woman back safely.

The smell of coffee ends my silence after my prayer. I get up from the floor and head to the kitchen to make a cup to start my day. A weird sensation comes over me suddenly and my breath catches. I grab the counter and stand still for a moment. "That was fucking weird." I call out to no one. I wait for the feeling to pass, finish with my coffee and head to the bathroom. *A nice hot shower to limber me up and get me moving.* Something has to give with this case. I need to find Mel.

Sitting at my table in front of my laptop I'm reading a few emails, checking in, and following up on new leads of Mel's whereabouts. Even though I'm on my third cup of coffee, since I've showered, I've only got as far as putting on a clean pair of jeans. Stretching and leaning back, I look at the clock. It's almost noon.

I haven't heard from Gabe yet today. I suppose I should get off my ass and head over there to see what's what on his end. Belle hasn't been doing so good since Mel went missing. It's like a piece of her went missing too.

I close my laptop and pack up everything I need in my duffle bag. I head into my bedroom and go right to my dresser. I pull out some socks and a tee shirt. I look in the mirror at my brown shaggy hair and run my fingers through it. Good enough. I pull my grey tee over my head and down my body and then sit on the side of my bed to put my socks on. My cell rings as I finish. It's Gabe.

"Hey, I was just thinking about you." I chuckle as I stand and head back out to the living room.

"Got no time to joke around man. A Jane Doe was just admitted to the hospital that Belle works at. Meet us there." Gabe tells me bluntly.

Shock hits hard and my heart begins to race. *Can it be her?* "See you in ten." I hang up, put on my shoes and grab my bag to go. With my keys in hand, I'm out the door with high hopes and wishful thinking.

CHAPTER FIVE

Mel

Everything hurts. My head, my face, my chest, everything. I try opening my eyes. It's too bright so I close them again. My throat is dry. I swallow, but it feels like sandpaper. I try to ask for water, but I can't open my mouth. Panic hits. Why can't I open my mouth? Slow breaths in through my nose. I try to stay calm. I open my eyes slowly and let them adjust to the light and look around. I'm in a hospital? Why? What happened to me? I hear beeping and look over my shoulders to monitors with wires that seem to be connected to me. A pole holding a bag of liquid that also seems to run a line connected to my arm. I look at my arm covered in bruises and a large bandage at my shoulder, and at the other which is covered in the same. I wonder what the rest of me looks like. I try calling out again forgetting I can't talk, my mouth won't open and it hurts like hell. Tears start to fall down my face.

Confused and frustrated, I toss the blankets aside and begin to move to sit on the side of the bed. The wires that are stuck to my body pull and some disconnect. Alarms start beeping, but I press forward. A door flies open and a flurry of people rush in.

"Miss, please stay in the bed." One young blonde nurse says to me as she silences the alarms.

A young dark haired man is instantly by my side. "Let me help you back. Less strain for you." And as if I was a just a feather, the man swoops his arms under my knees and wraps an arm around my shoulders and swings me back around. Everything goes so fast, I didn't have time to settle my own mind.

Grumbling behind my tight-lipped mouth, I try to express concern of my situation. I want to know what is going on. Looking around from nurse to what I must assume is an orderly, the looks of confusion they display frustrate me more. More tears start to fall.

"Jane, I will have the doctor come in and talk to you. I'm sure you are wondering about the extent of your injuries. Just give me a moment." She rechecks all the equipment and walks out the door.

Jane? That's not my name, is it? I try to really think about it…what *is* my name? I stop breathing as shock kicks in. Tears dry up and I huff out a slow breath so I can breathe. "This isn't good." I mumble out loud (incoherently through locked teeth.) I don't know who I am. And I can't talk. This totally sucks.

There's a knock on the door and in walks a short, grey haired man with dark rimmed glasses. "Good afternoon, Miss. I'm Dr. Horsley." He comes to the side of my bed and sits in the chair that's there. "I hear you've been a bit anxious." He opens the chart he has in his lap and starts to flip the pages. "I'm sure you'd like to know what's going on." He stops page-flipping and looks at me.

I look at the older gentleman, sniff my remaining tears back, and nod. I take a slow deep breath in through my nose while I wait to hear what my poor body and mind has been through.

"Well, Miss, you were found beside a dumpster at the back of the grocery store just down the street here. To be honest, you were a bloody mess." He shakes his head and looks at me with grim face. "You were barely breathing. The store manager just happened to park behind the store, so he's the one who found you and called for help."

I blink a couple times at him, staring sort of blankly then nod for him to go on.

He returns the nod and continues. "After assessing you for your injuries we noted several bruises, cuts, and bumps. On your upper arm, it appears you were grazed by a bullet, the wound was deep, but we fixed that up... You have a contusion on your clavicle which will heal on its own and you have a few cracked ribs." Dr. Horsley clears his throat. "And the biggest of all is that broken jaw of yours. Well, not completely broken—you have what is called a condyle fracture. We had to fix that up and wire you shut." He looks at the page in the chart. "Now all we need from you is a name. So, little lady, do you have a name?" He smiles a small smile for me.

Cracked ribs and a contusion on my clavicle. What the—contusion on my clavicle? I was shot at?

I shrug my shoulders at him and feel a slight twinge of pain in the space between my neck and shoulder. I didn't notice it earlier. Maybe now that I'm aware of my injuries I'm feeling them.

Dr. Horsley narrows his eyes. "What are you shrugging your shoulders for? You don't know your name?"

I shake my head no to the now confused doctor.

He flips through a few more pages and stands up. "Well, this isn't good. I think we need to repeat your head scan and do more blood work. You didn't present with a concussion, so I'll get things checked so we can be sure everything is okay. I'm sure your memory will come back very soon. Stress and pain can do many things to the mind." He starts toward the door and looks over his shoulder. "There's a button on the rail to the left of you. If you need something, you press it and someone will come help you out. I'll be back later, after the scan and blood work has been done. Take care, Miss."

I have a fractured jaw. My mouth is wired shut. Cracked ribs and a contusion on my clavicle. What the heck happened to me? If I only had my memory, then I'd have answers.

A few minutes later the same orderly from earlier comes in and hooks me up to portable monitors. I must be going down for my scan now. I watch the guy do everything. It's not like I have anything else to do (beside deal with the pain) and then we're on the move.

Back in my room the nurse draws some blood from me to do some tests and gives me an injection to help with my pain. The meds are working fast. I'm feeling groggy and pain free. I think a little nap is in order. Maybe I'll dream of who I really am.

I'm woken to the door being shoved open and slammed against the wall.

CIRCUMSTANCES UNRAVELED

CHAPTER SIX
Jack

I'm at the hospital in seven minutes. I drive right over the curb, not giving a damn about anything else right now but Mel. I slam on the brakes once I pull into a spot and shove my gears into park. I shut the ignition off, snag my keys, jump out, and rush in the emergency room waiting area to find Gabe and Belle.

They're standing just offside to the nurse's desk. Belle seems to be waiting to talk to a co-worker. I rush up to them. "Is it her?" I blurt.

Gabe puts his hands on my shoulders and holds me still. "We're still trying to find out. Calm down. Belle's freaked out, too. Take a deep breath, man. You seem worked up." He gives me a slight squeeze on the arms and lets me go.

I blow out a breath. "Yeah, I am sort of worked up. I'm pumped to kick some ass. I want to find out who took her and take some anger out on them." I start to pace in front of him.

"You have feelings for our girl, Jack? Something you're not telling me?" Gabe asks with a smile in his voice.

I stop and look at him. "Shut up." I grimace. "Now's not the time to discuss it, but yes." I look to Belle and see she's finally talking to someone. Gabe must notice since he gives me a shove and we both move toward her.

When we stop, Belle turns to us. "Well?" We both spit out.

Belle licks her lips and a single tear runs down her cheek. "The Jane Doe is up in the Surgery Ward. Let's go." She wipes her face and grabs Gabe's hand.

Belle directs us up to the Surgery Ward and talks to the nurse in charge. The doctor on call has a do-not-disturb note on the patient file, but after Belle talks with the nurse, she peeks in the room. It's Mel. She identifies Jane Doe as Mel Snow to the staff and we go in. Apparently no one knew who Mel was because she's so banged up, so now the nurse calls the doctor to make him aware that the patient is one of their own.

With the room number known, I run down the hall to find the room. I push the door open and rush in with Belle and Gabe right behind. The sight before me will haunt my dreams for a very long time.

Mel's unrecognizable. Her face is so battered, bruised, and swollen. Her sleek black hair is a rat's nest covered with blood and dirt, and there are tubes and wires everywhere. The eyes that look up instantly at me are blank and scared, my heart sinks. My firecracker is broken.

Belle rushes right past me and stops at the end of the bed. Gabe stops beside me. Mel stares blankly at us all not speaking or moving.

I move to the end of the bed and Mel's head whips around to look at me. Fear is now plastered across her face. Gabe walks over to Belle and wraps an arm around her shoulder for comfort.

"Mel, who did this to you?" Belle questions her. She doesn't see the fear like I do. She hasn't noticed that Mel doesn't recognize us.

I swallow a thick lump as my stomach sinks. I look to Belle and Gabe and back to my broken girl. "Do you know who we are?" I simply ask as I look directly at Mel with a calm face.

Belle blurts out immediately. "Of course, she knows us, Jack. She's my best friend. She knows who I am. Why would you say that?" She looks to me with a stern look and then back to Mel with raised eyebrows waiting for her answer.

Gabe catches on to what I'm thinking and watches Mel's expressions. I think he understands. He touches Belle's shoulder to get her attention and she looks to him. He frowns. "Mel is suffering memory loss, babe. Amnesia."

Belle slumps into Gabe's arms as tears start to roll down her face. "No…"

"I'm sorry, Belle. We'll have to talk to the doctors about it." I look to Mel again. She watches us, taking it all in. Her poor busted face. She still hasn't said anything. I don't understand why.

Gabe moves to sit in the chair in the corner with Belle in his lap, holding her, comforting her while she cries out her frustration.

I move to the side of the bed as Mel watches me. Machines start to beep loudly. I look and see her heart rate is increasing. I'm scaring her. Shit. "Please don't be afraid of me. I mean you no harm." I wave my hand toward Belle and Gabe. "That woman over there's your best friend, Isabelle. We call her Belle for short. The man is Gabe, her boyfriend. He is your friend, too." I pull a chair from behind me closer so I can sit and watch the monitor. Her heart rate is slowing down. "I'm Jack. I'm also your friend. We've been looking for you for almost three weeks now. Do you understand?" I ask. I need her to answer. She has yet to speak, so unless something has happened, she should. She was a spitfire of a talker before.

"Hmph." She muffles and I don't understand. She barely moved her mouth. What's going on?

"I'm sorry, I didn't catch that."

A tear rolls down her cheek and she opens her lips to show me the problem. Metal. She has metal in her mouth. Oh, fuck. Her jaw must be broken or something, and it's wired shut. That explains it.

"I understand." I reach for her closest hand, but she pulls back. "It's okay. I just want to let you know you're safe. But I understand." I pull my hand back and put it in my own lap.

"Why isn't she talking to you, Jack?" Belle asks from across the room.

I look over to her and see her wiping her damp, redden face. "She has a broken jaw—I think—and her mouth is wired shut."

The tears start to run down Belles cheeks again and Gabe pulls her in close. We need to get more answers about Mel's injuries. I doubt the nurses will give us those answers, so we'll sit here until the doctor comes. Then I'm going to keep searching for the bastards that did this to her.

CIRCUMSTANCES UNRAVELED

CHAPTER SEVEN
Mel

These three people say they are my friends, but they don't look familiar at all—Belle, Gabe, and Jack. I don't recognize the names, either. The woman, Belle, seems to be taking things hard, so I must be something to her...but what?

They keep calling me Mel. That name sounds a little more familiar than Jane. I try to search my mind to see if anything pops up when I say the name a couple times. After the third time, a different name popped in my mind. *Sydney. Where did that come from?* I try and say Mel a few more times in my mind and the name Sydney comes again. I shake my head and frown.

"Are you okay, Mel?" The guy—Jack—asks from beside me. I forgot for a minute that he was there.

I turn my head to look and nod. I point to the cup of water with a straw on the stand beside him. I'm so dry. I could drink anything right now. He reaches over, grabs it, and hands it to me. I maneuver the straw in between my cheek and teeth and try to suck. I get a little water, but mostly drool the water down my chin.

Jack moves quick to grab some tissues to clean up the spilled liquid. He wipes my chin and man does that ever feel weird. I pull back and look at him.

He smiles apologetically. "Sorry, just trying to help."

I don't know what to say to him. Heck, I can't talk to him, so I just nod. I still feel dry and try to sip again with better luck. I hand him the cup and he puts it back on the stand.

I look over to my other company and see the woman, Belle, asleep. Poor girl, she cried herself out. The man, Gabe, is caressing her hair, taking care of her. How sweet. I hope to have that someday.

Pain starts to return. I don't know how long it's been since I had medicine for it. I look around to see where the doctor told me to push a button for help. Oh, there it is. A button on the rail. I push it and a few minutes later a nurse comes in.

The nurse looks around the room with a smile and stops at the end of the bed. "What can I help you with, my dear?" She asks.

"Hrm." I try to get out that I'm in pain.

The nurse grimaces. "Are you having pain?"

I immediately nod and she smiles.

"I'll go get you something for that right now. Be right back." The nurse walks out leaving the door open for immediate return.

"Can I do anything for you?" Jack asks me.

I don't want the man doing everything for me and since the nurse is taking care of my medical needs, I think I'm good for now. I look to him and shake my head. He nods his head and sits back in his chair.

My company is pretty determined to stick around for me. Maybe they're waiting to talk to the doctor, or something. The man Gabe is now sleeping, the pair of them in the one chair doesn't look to comfortable, but maybe that's what love is. Someday, maybe.

I see the nurse in my peripheral vision as she comes in and watch her move to my intravenous. She has a needle in her hand. "This is a little morphine for you. It will make you drowsy, so don't feel you need to stay awake." She plunges the medicine into the port and then disposes of the needle.

"I'll make sure she rests." Jack speaks up and smiles at the nurse. "Thanks."

I can feel the morphine slowly starting to work. The pain begins to fade and I get sleepy. I want to stay awake to talk to the doctor when he comes in. I've had my scan and blood work and he said he'd be back. But my eyelids start to get very heavy.

"Sleep, my little firecracker. Sleep." Jack whispers.

I close my eyes.

I'm running down a hallway, being chased. Looking back a tall heavy set man is pursuing me. I need to get away from him. Something isn't right. My arm's really sore. I'm crying. I pass by a mirror and see a young teen aged version of me. A voice is yelling from behind me.

"Sydney, unless you want to end up like your mother you'll stop fucking running from me, you little bitch."

I can't look back again. I know he's getting closer. I have to get out of the house. I don't want to end up like mom. Dad just stabbed mom to death in their bedroom. I heard them arguing and I just wanted them to stop. I shouldn't have gone in.

Keep running, Sydney. The end of the hall's close. Then the stairs and the front door. I can do it.

I trip on the bottom step, screaming out in the pain. My arm is broken. Dad threw me against the wall and I heard a snap. He was going to do more—I know he was, but I ran.

"Sydney Jane Waters. If you leave this house I'll find you. You can bet your life on it." My father yells as I whip open the door and keep running. Until I run into Sebastian, my father's driver.

I wake to the soft talking in the room. Off to the side are Belle, Gabe, and Jack. Talking with them is the doctor. I hear him explaining my injuries, the same as he explained to me. But then he starts talking about my scans. Wait, I want to know about those. I growl and they turn towards me.

"Oh, you are awake. That's great." Dr. Horsley says as he walks to me.

Everyone follows. Jack returns to his chair and Belle and Gabe stand at the end of the bed.

"I was just about to tell your friends about your recent scans. I know you'll have questions." He looks around the room for something and shakes his head. "We'll have to get something for you to write on. I apologize for not thinking of that before now." He frowns. "For now, if you don't mind, you can just listen and when we get the supplies, you can ask all the questions you need." He raises his eyebrows and I nod to show I agree. "It looks like your amnesia is related to a possible concussion, so it should be short term. Your memory should come back soon, but don't rush it." He looks to me with a smile. "With amnesia, returning memories can be traumatizing, so make sure you keep your friends close. A support system is good for you right now. As for the rest of your injuries, your ribs will take time to heal. We can unwire your jaw in a few weeks as long as no further damage is done. Your blood work came back clean which is good. So, let's take one day at a time, shall we?" He shakes Jack's hand and Gabe's and nods to Belle before he leaves.

I half-listen to what the doctor said. My dream's still playing over in my mind. That's twice now that the name Sydney has come to my consciousness. But now a full name. Sydney Jane Waters. That must be my name, not Mel. If so, who are these people talking about?

CIRCUMSTANCES UNRAVELED

CHAPTER EIGHT

Jack

"That's great news—right, Gabe? Mel will get her memories back soon." Belle asks Gabe and looks to me. "We just have to be patient. Then she can tell us who did this to her." Belle turns and hugs Gabe.

Until her jaw is unwired, we need a way to communicate with her. My poor woman must be frustrated not being able to talk. "I'm going down to the gift shop to get a note pad and pen for her so she can talk with us." I smile at Mel. "I'll be right back."

As I head to the elevator I think back to what the doctor said. Her memory will come back. Thank Christ for that. I can't lose her. I want all of this woman, body, soul, and mind. I only get one chance at this. At love, that's all I'll allow myself and I want it with Mel. The doors open for the elevator and I enter. Reading the list, I find which floor the gift shop is on and hit floor one and wait.

Exiting on the first floor, I follow the signs to the shop. Along the way I notice a Timmie's and stop to grab coffee for everyone. I'm sure Belle and Gabe are just as exhausted as I am and a little pick-me-up can't hurt.

With a tray of coffee in hand, I head to the gift shop and find what I'm looking for—a simple note pad and a small package of pens—and pay. The less time I spend away from Mel, the better. Plus, I want to ask Belle about the supposed other men from her rape case, so I can look into them.

Back at the room, Mel's asleep again. The pain meds are doing a good job. Gabe and Belle sit in the corner again, so I head over to them. I hand them their hot beverages and sit on the window ledge, setting the note pad and pens beside me. I turn to Belle and start my line of questioning. "Belle, can I ask you some things about the past?" I know it's a touchy subject, but if it's something that can help things now, I think we need to know.

She bites her bottom lip before she nods. "Sure."

"The men who hurt you in college, are they all out of prison?"

Belle looks to Gabe. I note the hurt in her eyes. "Yes, they were released before Mike was, I think." She starts to nibble on her lip again, a nervous habit I believe Gabe's mentioned before.

I look at our sleeping girl and shake my head. Could it be them? Can a man be that cruel? I answer myself instantly—yes, they can. "Can you tell me their names?"

I notice Belle tense up. Gabe must too because he wraps his arms around her. She swallows deep. "Riley... Riley Daniels and Matt Boomer, no Booker. Yeah, that's it. They were Mike's frat brothers."

"Booker and Daniels. Got it. Thanks. I'm going to look into them and see if they're in the area." I shift on the ledge and sip on my coffee. "Did you two want to head home and get some rest? I'll stick around here for a while." I ask.

Belle glances at Gabe and he brushes her hair out of her face. "We should go rest. You look exhausted, babe. We can come back later." Gabe says.

"Okay, a nap in a bed does sound good." She stands and turns to me. "You stay by her side, Jack. Don't let anything happen to her." Belle tells me with warning, but also with worry etched on her face.

I move to sit in the chair beside the bed and set my coffee down. "I won't let anything or anyone get to her. I swear, Belle." I smile to her.

I sit here and stare at my woman. She doesn't know it yet, but yes. She's my woman. Her swollen, black and blue face makes me angry, but also makes my heart hurt. It hurts for Mel and all she went through. I can't imagine it. I've yet to see under the blankets. The doctor mentioned cracked ribs and lots of bruising, but to what extent? Suddenly, a thought comes to mind.

Rape.

Was she raped?

The doctor didn't mention anything about sexual assault. My heart begins to race. I want to check. I want to throw the blankets off and assess her thighs. I want to check for damage. But I can't, that's crossing a line. A line I legally can't cross for many reasons. I clench my eyes shut and pray to God that Mel didn't suffer such abuse. What I see of her now is enough. If she was raped, I don't know how I'll be able to control my anger.

I pull my cell out of my pocket and search my contacts. I have a guy who can help me out and get things moving. I find his name and press dial.

"Dex? Jack here. On a case and need a work up done."

"Jack, my man, how are you?" My old acquaintance asks.

"Not good, Dex. Not good. My woman. She's been hurt. I need answers. Can you help me out?" I blow out a breath and pray he won't let me down.

"Your woman, eh? Sure. Where? The works?" He asks me if I need the full rape kit, and a DNA kit brought in. The works is what we used to call it back when we worked together.

"Yeah, man. If you can."

"Where you at?"

I glance over at Mel to make sure she's still sleeping and when I see she is, I keep talking. "I'm in Toronto man. Text me when you're in the area and I'll text you the details."

"Sounds good, Jack. I'll see you soon." Dex hangs up before I do.

I just sit there with my phone to my ear for moment. I'm going to get answers. I've never taken care of a woman before, but I'll do everything in my power to do right by this one.

CHAPTER NINE
Mel

I must've fallen asleep again. Those drugs are strong. I hear voices surrounding me, so I open my eyes and see new people in my room. Two females wearing scrubs, but their name tags say CSIS on them. One big stalky guy is also in the room. He's talking to Jack.

Jack.

I'm glad he's still around. I don't think I can tolerate so many strangers at once. The male's tag also says CSIS. What does the CSIS want with me?

I bang on the rail to get Jack's attention and wave my arm around to the new company in the room. I shrug my shoulders and shake my head to try to convey my question. I'm learning not to use my mouth, because every time I try it hurts.

Jack stops talking to the man and looks to me. He must notice my distress and walks over to me. "Hey. Sorry if we woke you." He begins to point to the new people and explains who they are. "This is special agent Darrell Blake. I asked him to help out with your case. Since I want to be by your side helping you, but I want to find the bastards who did this to you, Darrell's stepping in to be my right hand." He smiles and points to the two women who are watching me with what looks like sympathy. Even though I don't want their pity, I just return a blank stare. "These ladies are, Tosh and Jane. They're medical staff from the bureau here to help do some tests in hopes that we get some unanswered questions answered. The tests are sensitive in nature and I don't want to alarm you. I'll be here with you if you would like. But, we need to test to see if you were raped. To see if any DNA has been left behind." He reaches for my hand, but stops midway, looking for permission I assume. I feel this pull come from him. It's different and strange. I can't help but reach for him and take hold of his hand. I try to smile, but it doesn't turn out perfectly and it hurts. "Would it be alright if we do these tests?" He asks. Looking into his dark brown, hypnotizing eyes, how can I refuse? I nod.

Jack leans over me and kisses the top of my head. A warm feeling comes over me and I know I'm blushing, although he probably can't tell with all the bruising. Not that I can remember, but I don't think I've blushed from a simple kiss on the head before. I like it. I hope he does it again—and soon.

I haven't looked at a clock in a while, but it feels like a few hours have passed. The medical staff from the CSIS took samples from under my nails, picked blood and fibers from my hair, did a few swabs in and around my private areas, and took several photos. It exhausted me, but I'm glad it's over. I hope that Jack and his associate get the answers they are looking for.

64

It's only Jack and me here now. He sets a note pad and some pens in my lap.

"I got you these so we can communicate. You know, so you can answer questions or ask me things. That is, if you want." He raises his eyebrows and grins. "I want to cause as little pain as possible for you, so I thought this was the easiest way."

I see the pack of pens is already open and reach for them to take one out. Taking them both, I start to write.

Thank you, Jack.

"You're welcome, beautiful girl." He responds and I attempt to smile again.

There's something about this man, a connection of sorts. I feel comfortable with him. I don't understand why, but I'm not going to stop the feelings that are building in such a short time.

Will it take long to get results? I write and look to him.

"We're putting a rush on them, so it should only take a few days. After that, hopefully we will catch the people responsible for doing this to you."

I nod and look back down at my lap and write again. *So, we wait. Just like I wait and see if I remember who I am.*

Jack looks down just as I look up and our eyes meet. His eyes shine bright and I can't help but feel like he's looking into my soul. He glances to the note pad and reads. "Right." He answers. "Hopefully you get your memory back soon. I really want you to remember me." His eyes return to mine and my heart skips a beat.

The monitor beeps suddenly and stops. We both ignore it and just stare at each other.

Does he feel it, too?

Belle and Gabe interrupt us. Looking fresh, both with smiles on their faces, they come in carrying flowers and a teddy bear that says get well.

I huff out the breath I didn't realize I was holding while being held hypnotized in Jack's eyes and turn my attention to my guests. I smile at them and start to write something. *Hi. Welcome back.*

Belle turns just in time to see me lift the note and smiles. "Thanks. I hope you're feeling a little better."

Gabe smiles at me and walks over to Jack. "Why don't you take a few hours and go get something to eat and freshened up. Let us take a shift. We got this for a bit." He tells him as he puts a hand on Jacks shoulder and raises his eye brows.

Jack puts his hand on top of Gabe's and nods. "I think I will. Food and coffee sound good. I want to grab my laptop too, so it works out good that you're back." Jack steps over to me and leans down to kiss the top of my head. Heat rushes through me and I close my eyes. "I won't be long. Will you be okay?" He asks me. I look to Belle who watches me with a smile, holding a teddy bear, and then to Gabe who now holds Belle's hand in a reassuring way. Finally I face Jack and nod. With that, Jack turns and heads out of the room. I look back at my company and wait to see what they have for me.

JEAN KELSO

CHAPTER TEN
Jack

As soon as I'm in my truck, I pull out my cell. "Dex, it's me again, Jack. I just wanted to thank you for the help today."

"Your woman looked pretty rough, man. I'm glad I'm able to help." Dex tells me.

"For sure she does. I want to kill whoever did this to her. How long for results, man?" I ask as I stick my keys in the ignition and start my truck.

"I put a rush on everything like we discussed—so twenty-four to thirty-six hours tops. I wish we could get instant answers, man, but science isn't that quick."

Boy, do I wish science *was* that quick, but I know it doesn't work that way. Crimes would be solved so much faster if it did. "No, that's great, Dex. Thanks. I'll talk with you soon. Later, man."

"Hang tight, Jack. Bye."

I pull out of the hospital parking lot and go in search of food. I need to fill this empty feeling that resides in me and need to fuel my body and mind, so I'm strong enough to handle anything that comes our way while Mel's on the mend.

I drive around until I find a steak house. Some protein is just what I need. I pull in and park. I check the time and see I've been gone for twenty minutes already. Damn, time flies fast when you don't really want it to. I hop out of my truck and head in to grab some food.

The hostess seats me in a corner booth and hands me a menu. A waitress is by my side immediately, so I order a beer on tap and she walks away. I don't need to look at the menu. I already know what I want. I'm a meat and tater kind of guy and that's just what I'm ordering.

The waitress is back with my beer and I take a moment to take her in. She's tall with red curly hair. She has curves that go on forever, just what I used to go for in a woman, but not anymore. I hear a voice talking and I realize it's her.

"Have you decided?" The redhead asks while holding a note pad and pencil.

I nod and smile. "Yes, I have. I would like a T-bone, medium rare with a baked potato and whatever vegetable you have on today. Thanks." I tell her.

She's quick to scribble it down and nods. "I'll be back when it's ready, sir." She grins and saunters off.

Nope, not anymore. I chuckle to myself. Those days are over. I found the woman I want. I want Mel. I want my firecracker. She's hot and sassy—and hopefully soon I'll find out if she is sweet or spicy.

My mind starts to trail off to back at the hospital. My little endearment. My kiss on the head. I tried to stop myself, but I couldn't. I had to touch her with my lips. I had to feel her with my hand. The sizzling feeling I felt was shocking. I needed more. I swear when I kissed her, I felt heat radiate between us. Now I don't figure she had a fever, so either Mel was blushing something fierce, or I'm just damn crazy.

And the second time I did it (you know I'm just a sucker) I had to see if it would happen again. Plus, there's this invisible voice calling to me, daring me, so how could I not? And you know what? That heat was there again. I felt it. I felt something that is for damn sure. Mel may not remember me, but I damn well know there's a connection there between us and I'm not letting it go.

I think back to when I saw her at the coffee shop, her beautiful, black hair hanging loose down her back as she sat at a table all on her own. I wanted to sit with her, chat with her, get to know more about her, but I was afraid my chance was gone.

The red-headed waitress shocks me from my daydream and sets my meal in front of me. A bottle of hot sauce and extra napkins are also set on the table. "Enjoy your meal." She tells me with a knowing smile and a telling wink before she meanders off.

I ignore her flirty ways and unwrap my utensils. The deep smoky smell coming from my plate is making my mouth water. There's nothing better than a good chunk of steak. What am I saying? A damn fine woman is better, but I don't have that right now, so the meat will be my guilty pleasure.

I take another deep sniff and slice off a hunk. Shoving the meat in my mouth I cut off another piece and start cutting up my beautifully baked potato with all the fixings.

The atmosphere gets louder and the restaurant begins to get busy. I finish my last bite and sit back. With my beer in hand I take in the scenery, noting families and many couples. My gaze stops at a young couple sitting just a few tables from me. They must be waiting for their dinner. Their arms are resting on the table with their hands holding each other. I see their mouths moving—so they're talking—but it's their look. The way they look at each other. They love each other, I can see it. I can't help but smile.

I want that.

Love.

I want to feel that, share it and do everything that comes with it. If I close my eyes I can picture Mel and I like that, sharing our time together, holding hands, being intimate.

I shake my head and see my waitress approach. She's smiling, of course. "All finished?" She licks her lips and blinks several times, batting her long lashes, probably trying to get my attention. Something she could get from any man, but not me.

"Sure am. Can I have my bill, please?" I ask her politely and reach in my pocket for my wallet. I notice her pout as she sees I'm not falling for her little act.

She sets the little piece of paper on my table, grabs my plate, and starts to walk away. I can hear little mumbles as she walks and I have to chuckle. The poor girl's trying too hard and going for the wrong man. But of course, I'm not saying anything.

I stand up, grab my bill and head to the front to pay.

CHAPTER ELEVEN
Mel

The kids at school are all pointing, staring at me and laughing. Shame warms my skin. I hold my math books close and head to class.

My teacher, Mr. Landers asks if I'm alright when I enter. I nod my head and go to my seat. It's the last class of the day, I just want to get it over with and get home. If I'm late again, who knows what dad will do.

The bell rings. I gather my stuff and go to my locker. I pack my bag, put on my jacket, and rush out the door.

We don't live far from the school, but dad said he will be waiting for me and I don't want to disappoint him. I look both ways before I cross the road and begin to run.

I hurry in the door and look at the time. I blow out a breath, thankful I made it home in time.

"Sydney, that better be you." My dad bellows as he comes down the hall.

I tremble with fear as I take off my jacket and set my bag down. "Yes, dad. I'm home."

He enters the foyer and looks me up and down. "You are very lucky, little one. Did anyone question your black eye?" He narrows his dark, thick eye brows and looks sternly at me.

71

Standing still and as calm as I can, I answer. "I told them I tripped and hit my face on the door knob, sir." I try hard not to be rude as I speak, but God forbid anyone finds out that my father, the senator, beats his child.

He growls his anger toward me. "If anyone comes knocking on my door about you Sydney..." He raises his hand...

I wake. I can't breathe. Alarms start sounding around me. I feel the bed move, sitting me up. A tube is wrapped around my face and a fresh slight breeze is forced in my nose. I open my eyes and see Jack. His face is etched with worry.

"It was just a dream, baby. Just breathe." Jack whispers to me as he pushes my tussled hair out of my face.

Baby? I try and shake the dream and just breathe as I'm told. Slow, deep breaths. The cool air coming in my nose is helping a lot and Jack caressing my head is relaxing me, too.

I've been in the hospital now for a week. It feels like longer, but no, only a week. Jack hasn't really left my side. Belle and Gabe come and go, but I know they both have jobs they need to be at. But Jack? I guess he works freelance, so he can work whenever.

The results from all the tests had come back and we got good news and bad. The good news was that the CSIS was able to get a hit off the DNA and now there are warrants of arrest for three men. Two of the men are the men that Gabe was talking about.

The bad news (which is part of the reason why Jack hasn't left my side) is that I was raped—and more than once apparently. When I was told this, I didn't know how to react. Shock was a big part and tears came. I can't fathom how people can treat others that way. But the look on Jack's face—the hurt, the pain—it's like he's being tortured for something I went through. In a way, I'm thankful that I can't remember, but then again how am I supposed to get over it, to deal with it, if I can't remember?

As I calm myself, I reach for my note pad. *Thank you.* I write to Jack.

He stops rubbing my head and reaches for the pad. He smiles as he looks to me. "I'll do anything to help. I won't let anything happen to you. Want to talk about the dream?" He asks and leans on the bed rail looking all sweet and sexy. Endearing and caring. His smell is divine and does things to me. Sexy things. I get this funny feeling in my belly and a tingly feeling in my private parts.

How is it that a man's smell can turn me on? Maybe it's just Jack, part of the connection that seems to be growing. Over this past week, I've noticed that when I first wake up he's the person I want to see, the first person whose voice I want hear. We must have a past, or present of sort. This memory thing is taking too long. I want to know who I am and what Jack is to me. Especially now that he's calling me "baby". I must mean something to him. I know I *want* to mean something to him.

I take the pad from him and have the urge to bite my lip, but not being able. Damn it, when will this wire crap come out?

I think my name's Sydney. I turn the pad to him, raising my eyebrows and hold my breath. I keep dreaming about this Sydney so that must be my name. It feels right, it sounds right.

He frowns as he reads it and shakes his head. "No. Your name is Melanie. We call you Mel for short."

I grunt, feeling frustrated. I stab the pen to the paper again and write. *In every dream, I have, I'm Sydney. It feels right. I'm Sydney!* I want to put a hundred exclamation marks to make my point, but I don't. I just turn the paper toward him and glare.

Jack immediately stands up and rubs his hand down his face. "I don't know what dreams you're having, baby. But, your name is Melanie Snow." He pulls his phone from his pocket and starts typing.

Frustration over takes me and tears pool and fall down my face. How can I have two names? I know my name's Sydney, but Jack's fighting me on it. I don't want to upset him. Damn you, memory, what are you doing to me?

Jack rushes to my side when he sees I'm crying. "Don't cry. Please, baby. I hate seeing you cry." He takes my hands in his and kisses the palms of both. I cry a little more. How sweet is this man? He holds my hands in his and gently rubs his thumbs over my knuckles. "Gabe and Belle will be here shortly. Maybe they can help with this little mix up."

I sniff my salty tears and blink a few times to hold the rest back. I nod my head in understanding. Then it hits me. My last name. I have a last name. I pull my hands free from him and grab the pad. *According to my dreams, my last name is Waters. If that helps.* I turn it to him and give him a small smile with hope.

"It just might. Thank you." He leans forward and kisses my forehead. I swoon for the man that keeps doing simple naughty things to me. A kiss on the head here, a gentle caress there. Story of an amnesiac falling in love. I laugh to myself and smile.

I try and clear my throat. It's very dry in this place. Jack hands me a cup of water with a straw and I gladly accept it. Over the past week, I have aced a maneuver on how to drink without spilling. I drink my fill and hand it back to him. All my tubes are gone and I'm only hooked up to a monitor for my vitals. I'm able to get out of bed and walk around. I have showered once with the help of a nurse and it felt amazing. Belle brought in a suitcase with a bunch of my stuff so now I'm able to wear my own clothes and brush my hair as well. After getting my hair washed, getting all the blood and dirt free from the rat's nest, pulling a brush through my long locks felt heavenly.

The swelling has decreased on my face, so has the bruising. You can actually make out cheek bones and see my actual eyes. My ribs still hurt, but not as much. My arms and legs are marked with yellowish green spots as the bruising fades from them as well. All in all, things are looking up. Now I just need my jaw to heal so they can take the stupid metal out. Keeping my teeth clean and my mouth fresh is near to impossible. I can just imagine what Jack thinks when he gets close enough to smell me.

CHAPTER TWELVE
Jack

Mel's doing a word search I bought her and I'm checking my emails on my laptop when Gabe and Belle walk in. A tray of coffee in hand and what looks like a box of donuts from Timmie's. Score. I could go for a nice sweet treat right about now. Gabe hands me my large coffee, then hands Mel an iced coffee. I don't know how anyone can drink cold coffee, but it's something Mel loved to drink before all this. She hasn't complained yet, so to each their own. Gabe and Belle then go and sit in the other chairs with their hot beverages.

The smell of the coffee is intoxicating, I can't help but start drinking it. It's hot as hell, but I need a caffeine fix. After my first sip, I sigh. Everyone in the room laughs, even Mel, well as best as she can. I didn't realize how loud I was. "What? Can't a man enjoy a good cup of coffee?" I smirk and shake my head.

Belle starts right in. "So, Jack says you had another dream, Mel?" Damn woman couldn't just ease in, could she?

I hear the breath Mel takes and watch her look to Belle and nod. She then scrambles through her notes and holds up the piece of paper that mentions her name. *I think my name is Sydney.*

I watch Belle read it and then look at me, questions beaming at me with no words.

Mel starts to scribble on paper and holds it to Belle again. *Sydney Waters.*

I've never seen anyone look dumbfounded before, but if I was to ever see it, now would be it. Belle looks so lost and dumbfounded. "What do you mean your name is Sydney Waters? Your name has been Mel Snow for the entire time I've known you." She looks to Gabe and then to me again. "Jack? What does this mean?" She asks.

"Mel's been having these weird dreams, sometimes scary ones, over the past week. In every one her name is Sydney Waters. I don't know if they're memories or what. I have emailed my source with the CSIS and they are checking the name out for me. I hope to get an answer back soon."

Gabe reaches for Belles hand and frowns. "How can she be two people? I mean, her memory is supposed to come back, but she isn't remembering who she is." Gabe growls. "Fuck, I mean, is she remembering someone else's memories? Is Mel not Mel?"

Frustrated with the whole situation, my patience running thin, I hit refresh on my email with hopes of answers. "Gabe, man. She's still the same woman. Fuck." I return his growl just as my email pings.

I look down to see that Dex has done his job well. I hit the attachment that is with the email and my jaw drops. It's an obituary notice from Washington, DC.

Sydney Jane Waters

78

Age 15

Daughter of Senator Douglas Waters and Marsha Waters(deceased)

I stop reading and look to the photo. It's a spitting image of Mel, but younger and with blonde hair. No fucking way. Is it possible? I look over at Belle and Gabe and glance at Mel as she now sleeps peacefully.

What the hell is going on here? Is Mel really Sydney? My mind is spinning, searching for answers only that Mel or Sydney can give. I stand and walk over to Gabe and set my laptop in front of the pair. If I'm as shocked as I am, I can't imagine the reaction Belle will have.

"Oh, my God!" Belle shouts as she stands up and starts to pace. "No way! How is this possible?" She moves toward her friend and kneels beside the bed. "Why would she not tell me?"

Gabe stares at the screen, you can tell his mind is running a mile a minute by the way he clenches and unclenches his fist. He's thinking. He's probably thinking the same as me. "She's obviously hiding something huge, something that puts her in danger." He looks to me and then to his weeping woman crouched beside her best friend.

Following his gaze my heart thumps with wonderment and curiosity. What could be so bad that Mel would need to change her entire identity? I take my laptop and go sit back down beside the bed. I read over the email to see if any of the information can give a clue or two.

Pulling up a search bar, I do a search for Douglas Waters. Maybe if I had information on the man, dots will connect. As I read, I make quick note of some information that I think I'll need. *Mother found murdered in the home; house burglarized. Sydney missing and found dead less than a week later. Douglas Senator of Washington State for the past sixteen years. One scandal with a prostitute stating the Senator abused her.*

"Hey." Belle says and I look up. Mel is waking up. "Have a good rest?" It was a short nap, but she needed it.

Mel nods and smiles. She's getting better mouth control now that the swelling is going down. She looks around until she sees me. She stops and smiles bigger. Her eyes sparkle, shining bright as she stares momentarily.

I smile back. "Hey, you. I love seeing that smile." Instantly her cheeks flush. She reaches around on the bed for the note pad, once she has it she starts to scribble things down.

Thank you. Why does Gabe look so serious?

She nods toward Gabe and looks back at me while she hands me the note.

I didn't realize Gabe was still in his "think" mode, so I clear my throat to get his attention. He immediately averts his eyes to us. "Yeah?" He asks. He must have been in his own little world or something. When something is on his mind, when he is processing something, he tunes everything out.

"Just checking to see if you were with us, man." I chuckle and reach for Mel's hand.

He smiles and nods. "Yeah, sorry. Was just thinking."

I give Mel's hand a little squeeze. "Mel, I had my friend look into Sydney Waters."

CIRCUMSTANCES UNRAVELED

CHAPTER THIRTEEN
Sebastian

Washington, DC

My laptop pings with an alert notifying me of email. I move from my kitchen table to the living room where my computer sits. Opening my email I see one flagged. Why, I wonder. Clicking on the document, it opens and immediately my heart stops. It's a notification that the CSIS has done a check into Sydney Waters. Shit. This isn't good.

I remember the day I saw her run from the house, tears streaming down her face. Her arm was bent at an odd angle. I knew Douglas had a mean streak, but I never thought he'd hurt his family, so I followed Sydney. Once I caught up to her and calmed her down, I listened to what she had to say. My jaw dropped at it all. My loyalty was to the Senator, but there was no way I was letting his teenage daughter suffer. I gave her the cash I had on me and told her to go to a specific hotel and wait for me. I was going to confront the man who I thought was a true family man.

The Senator called and said there was a break in and he needed my help. I (of course) didn't believe him—not after seeing Sydney in such distress and hearing what she had to say. My loyalty to his cause took precedence, but not necessarily to the man himself. I was told that men broke in and attacked his wife and daughter. Douglas's story didn't match his daughter's. But I have two eyes and I believe what I see, so while still hesitant I helped deal with the situation.

I don't know what came over him, but he then put a hit on his own daughter. The senator went crazy. I did everything I could to stop him, to change his mind—even to figure out why he would do such a thing to his own family. I couldn't control my anger and shock. Douglas could tell I was ready to turn him in. Then came the threats. Death threats. I was only twenty years old, the youngest boy in the family. My mother depended on me for medical bills and what not. I wasn't ready to die. I wasn't ready for my parents or siblings to die. I was stuck. Nowhere to turn, nowhere to run. So, I swallowed what pride I had left in me and struck a deal with the devil of a man, the senator. Only, it wasn't a deal I planned to keep.

With help of a body from a mortuary and Sydney's car, I faked her death. I did what I could to fake all the documents to prove that it was her in the car.

Just because I signed my death warrant with the devil, doesn't mean I had to actually sign one for his innocent daughter.

With the senator happy that she was gone, I proceeded to getting Sydney a new identity and recommending where she should try going.

After I got her set up, I haven't seen her since. This is the first I've heard anything about her. This isn't how I wanted her to pop up.

I stand and start to pace the room. Something serious must have happened for the Canadian government to be looking into her through FBI alliances. I sit on the couch and look at the email again. It can't be real. Not possible. Sydney wouldn't screw things up. She wouldn't do anything to jeopardize her life or mine—I'd hope—especially when it comes to her father.

Shit. I stand again and clench my fists in frustration, pacing around the room. I should have ran away myself years ago, but I was scared. Douglas Waters has the means to harm so many people, it isn't even funny. I just hope he doesn't find out that I helped her escape or I'm dead.

My cell rings. I look at the ID and it's Douglas. I gasp. "Shit. He must know." If I don't answer, he'll think something is up.

I answer on the third ring. "Hello, sir, what can I help you with?" I do my best to contain the fear in my voice.

"How is that lovely daughter of yours, Sebastian? Well, I hope? I wouldn't want anything bad to happen to her, would you?" The senator says in a stern voice. A chill runs up my spine. Shit. No. I can't let him touch my little girl.

I take a deep breath and blow it out slowly. "She is great actually. Playing with the neighbor's kids right now." I know I'm kicking myself for asking, but I won't play games with him. Not now. "Why do you ask?"

A growl comes through the phone. "Let's talk emails." I hear teeth gritting. "Did you happen to get one recently that might upset me at all, Sebastian?"

I clench my eyes shut and calm my breathing before I speak. "I haven't checked my emails today, sir."

"DON'T FUCKING LIE TO ME!" Douglas yells and blows out a breath. "I know you read your emails."

I pull the phone away from my ear for a second and look up to my ceiling. I can't do this. I start pacing the floor again. Putting the phone back to my ear I start back in on his game. "Alright, sir. Yes, I've read my emails. What would you like to know?" I wait for more screaming, but it doesn't come. I get silence. "Sir?"

"You remember when your wife had that little car accident and didn't survive? What a tragedy it was."

I think for a moment. Why would he mention the accident? Then it dawns on me. It wasn't an accident. Fuck! My heart starts racing and I rush to my daughter's room and start packing some clothes.

"It wasn't an accident, was it, Douglas?" I grit my teeth and sneer. In return I get laughter. The little hairs on my neck stand and I don't know what to feel anymore, fear or anger, both maybe.

"Of course not, friend—and with what looks like my daughter being alive, you need to learn another lesson." The phone goes dead. I drop my phone, grab Lilly's back pack and head to my room to pack. I need to pack up the car and get the fuck out of dodge with my daughter. If I can, I'll find Sydney where I recommended her to run to and warn her.

CIRCUMSTANCES UNRAVELED

CHAPTER FOURTEEN
Mel

Looked into her? So…am I her or not? Tension builds inside of me. My mouth and throat get dry. I'm actually nervous to find out the answer.

Water, please. I scribble quickly on the paper and Belle hands me a cup with a straw to drink from. I take few soothing sips and swallow deeply. Handing the cup back to Belle, I put the pen to the paper again. *What did you find out?* I turn the paper to Jack and look to him as my anxiousness increases.

Jack sets his computer on the table beside the bed and takes hold of both my hands. I grab them like a lifeline. I'm eager to see if my dreams are just dreams, or if they're my reality. Jack glances to the others and back to me, looking a little unsure whether to answer me or not. I tip my head and squeeze his hands in encouragement. I need to know.

"Sydney Waters is dead, Mel." I don't let him finish speaking. That can't be true. I feel it in my bones that she is me. I mean, that I'm her.

I pull my hands from his and grab for the note pad. Scribbling as fast as the thoughts come. *You're wrong. I'm her. I know I am.* I look from Belle to Gabe and worry etches itself on both of their faces. They can't believe this, can they? I look back at Jack as tears roll slowly down my cheeks.

Jack takes my hands in his again. He leans down and kisses them, caressing my knuckles with his thumbs before he looks at me with sincerity. "Slow down, you. You didn't let me finish talking."

The asshat told me I'm dead, so yeah, I jump to conclusions. Who wouldn't? I press my lips tight and growl. My way of telling him to get talking.

He shakes his head at my growl. "Our firecracker is still in there." He chuckles and smirks. "Anyways, yes—an obituary was found, but the photo that is provided with the notice is a photo of you only younger. So we'll have to look further into this. Okay?" He raises his eyebrows in question.

I sniff back my sobs and wipe away my tears. I look like her, so all hopes are not dead yet. I nod in approval and smile.

Jack stands and leans over me and kisses my forehead. A tingly feeling is left where his lips touch. Every time he does something so sweet, I feel more and more for the man.

Everything feels heavy, my eyes are weighted down and I want to open them. I hear voices around me, calling my name. Telling me everything is okay. I swallow what little saliva I have and attempt to lick my lips, they are so dry. Anesthesia. That's what's wrong. I'm coming out of the anesthetic. I had my surgery to have my jaw unwired. The excitement of this runs through me and helps me open my eyes. Everything's blurry at first, but they're all here. Jack, Belle, and

Gabe. I smile as best as I can. I open my mouth and stick my tongue out a little. I don't know why, maybe just because I can. I hear laughter and turn toward it. Belle, she's giggling at my silliness.

I stick my tongue out again and cross my eyes looking down at my nose. Belle giggles again. I love the sound. It's comforting and familiar. Familiar? A stabbing pain shoots through my head. I squeeze my eyes shut for a moment, until the pain passes.

"Shit, are you okay, hon?" Belle asks as she takes my hand.

I nod a slow nod and open my eyes to her. I swallow again and try to talk. "Just a little pain." I manage to garble.

"She speaks. A wonderful sound it is." Jack says and Gabe agrees.

I turn my head to a smiling Jack. His smile is lazy, sexy and deliberate. It too is comforting to see. A sharp pain strikes my head again and I cringe. A flash of Jack and I talking in a coffee shop plays in my mind and then it's gone.

I blow out a breath and look at him. I'm starting to remember. I smile. He tips his head and raises his eyebrows. "Everything alright? That looked painful."

I nod my head quickly and answer. "I just had a memory."

Excitement and concern is expressed among all their faces. Jack reaches for my hand and squeezes it. "That's great."

"What did you see?" Belle asks.

"It was…"

CIRCUMSTANCES UNRAVELED

CHAPTER FIFTEEN
Jack

Mel's getting some of her memory back. That's great. I tell her so. I'm about to ask her what she remembers, but Belle beats me to it.

"What did you see?" Belle asks.

"It was…" Mel's eyes roll back and her whole body starts to tremble. Her arms and legs shake and drool is starting to come from her mouth. Shit. What's going on?

I jump from my chair. "Help. Can we get some help in here?"

Belle and Gabe move out of the way as nurses run in. Dr. Horsley rushes in right after them. "Stats?" He asks.

"Blood pressure is one eighty-seven over one hundred, pulse is one ten. She's seizing, doctor." One of the nurses assessing her calls out.

Dr. Horsley quickly looks her over and then to the monitors. "One milligram of Ativan IV push, stat." He looks to me, concern worn on his face. "Jack, is it?"

"Yes." I respond.

"What was going on before this happened?" He asks me.

I shrug my shoulders. "She said she had a memory. Her head hurt for a minute and that was it. I don't know what else to say." I lean against the wall, waiting, watching. My heart pounds so hard that it feels like it might pound right out of my chest.

The doctor nods and looks back over to Mel. Her body isn't shaking anymore. "The medicine's working. Thank you, ladies. Please check on her in an hour." He has the nurses leave and he turns back to me.

I, of course want to know what happened, so I ask. "What's going on, doc?"

Dr. Horsley looks around the room to make sure that Belle and Gabe are paying attention. "I was afraid of this. Her memories are returning."

I narrow my eyes, confusion apparent. "Is having her memories returning not a good thing?" I look to Gabe and Belle. They both look confused, just like me.

"Yes and no. Yes, because then she'll know who she is, past and present. No, for the fact that when all the memories come all at once that it can be very traumatic. I mentioned this a while ago. Her body and mind have been through so much already. The seizure is her body reacting to the overload of memories." He glances around the room, making his point across.

I take in what he says and put two and two together. It actually makes sense. It'd be a lot to process all at once. Does this mean that Mel knows who she is now? I guess we'll have to wait until she wakes up. "Thank you, Dr. Horsley. I understand what you're saying." I stick my hand out in request for a hand shake.

Dr. Horsley accepts and we shake hands. "No problem, Jack. The medicine should allow her to rest for a little while. When she wakes, truth will be told whether she has her memories back or not. If you need anything, have the nurses page me." He nods to us all and leaves the room.

I return to my chair beside the bed, as does Belle and Gabe.

After seeing my firecracker fizzle out, I'm a little on edge. I'm sure you would be too if you saw someone you love have their eyes roll back and whole body shake. So, now here we all sit, just watching over her, praying she wakes up and feels better. When Mel's body was trembling and the machines started beeping, I couldn't breathe. I didn't want to breathe. I have grown so attached to this woman and care for her more than she even realizes yet. I know it's strange considering I never used to be the loving man, but Mel? I'd hang the moon for her.

I hear moaning and immediately look up to see Mel's head moving back and forth on her pillow. I set the magazine down that I was reading and take hold of her hands. "Shhhh, baby. It's okay." I watch her as her head stills and her eyes slowly open.

She blinks a couple times, licks her dry lips and asks. "Jack? What happened?"

She tries to sit up, but instead I encourage her to lay still. "Lay still, Mel. You need to rest. You just had a seizure, so please lay still."

She clears her throat and looks over at me. Smiling a small grin, she ensures me she understands. "For you I will. I'm so glad you're here." She swallows. "I need a drink please."

I act fast and hand her a cup of ice water. She takes small sips, which I imagine feel wonderful on a dry throat. "Better?" I ask.

She nods. "Yes, thank you." I take the cup and set it back on the stand beside me. Mel looks around the room and returns her gaze to me, puzzled. "Where are Belle and Gabe?"

"They've gone to eat. They'll be back in a little while." I smile.

She reaches for the bed controls and sits herself up in the bed. Once Mel situates herself, she blows out a breath. "I remember, Jack." She whispers.

Her voice was so low I'm pretty sure I heard her right, but just in case I want her to repeat herself. "Say that again?"

"I remember. I remember everything." A lonely tear glides down her cheek. She moves quickly to wipe it away.

I stand and lean over her and kiss her forehead, pressing my lips and holding them to her skin for a moment longer than I need to—but I need to feel her. I drop my forehead to touch hers and look into her eyes. They shine bright, but I see worry. "That's great to hear, baby." I tell her.

Another tear leaks out. I reach up and wipe it away. "It is, but now I need to leave the city, Jack." She licks her lips and swallows.

What? Why? Why would she have to leave? What am I missing?

CHAPTER SIXTEEN
Mel

The confused look on his face crushes me. While not knowing who I was, having Jack by my side was everything. Getting to know him—all the sweet and kind gestures he did—I couldn't help but fall in love with the man. But now they know my real name. They used government contacts to search my real name and with that comes my father's ties. My father. A very powerful man—the senator of Washington—will search me out and finish what he started. I can't have that. I can't let anyone get hurt.

I cup my hand to Jack's cheek and run my thumb across it. Our eyes gaze into one another.

"Why? Why do you need to leave?" He asks. His tone's soft.

I drop my hand and look away. He has no choice but to pull back. He sits back on the chair. When I know he's sitting I look back. "My real name's Sydney Waters. Fifteen years ago I escaped from my father, changed my identity, and never looked back."

I watch him take in what I tell him. His eyes go from dull to bright to confused in the matter of minutes. I know I need to explain more of my situation to him—but I need to wait for Belle and Gabe to be here, so I don't need to explain it over and over.

He stands from the chair and walks to the window. Running his hand through his hair, he looks back to me. "I still don't understand, Mel. Explain to me why you need to leave, please." He leans against the window sill and crosses his feet in front of himself.

"Can you call Gabe and get him and Belle here so I can explain everything? I'd rather explain this once." Ugh, my jaw hurts. I touch my face and grimace. I look for my call bell and ring it. I think I'll need some pain medicine if I'm going to be talking so much.

Jack's eyes narrow when the nurse comes in. He must not have noticed me push the button while he was on the phone. "Are you in pain, Mel?" He watches as the nurse takes a needle and sticks my arm with it. He closes his eyes for a second and shakes his head. "Jesus. I'm sorry. I didn't think about this. Making you talk." He moves to my bedside and sits again. He waits for the nurse to leave and takes a hold of my hand closest to him.

Feeling the effects of the medicine, I start to relax. I'm not really good at handling narcotics, but I'm not going to let this dose pull me under. I want to stay awake and be with Jack. I want to spend as much time as I can with Jack before I have to run. "It's okay, Jack. I'll be fine. Are they coming?"

He nods. "Gabe said they'll be here in ten minutes." He leans down and kisses my hand. "Then I want to know everything. Okay?"

"Okay."

Almost to the minute, Belle and Gabe walk in with a tray of beverages. Concern mars both their faces as they hand both of us drinks and take a seat. I take a sip of my delicious iced coffee and lick my lips, moaning. "Yum." I say and everyone laughs.

"It's so great to hear you talking, Mel. We've missed that voice of yours." Belle grins as she opens her coffee and takes a small sip, being cautious not to burn herself.

"It feels great to talk again. It feels even better to know who I am." I bite my lip then smile.

Belle sets her coffee down and jumps from her chair rushing to me. She leans toward me, giving me a gentle hug. "Oh, hon! That's amazing news!" She pulls back. A tear runs down her cheek and she laughs lightly. "I have missed you like crazy, girl. I'm glad you're back."

"Thanks. It's great to be back...but I have things we need to talk about." I turn my happy face to a serious one and Belle returns to her seat.

Gabe takes ahold of her hand. "Jack mentioned something about that. Tell us what's going on." He stares at me intently.

I blow out a breath, look to Jack and reach for his hand. He's quick to respond and takes ahold of me. "Well...as I told Jack, I'm Sydney Waters."

Belle gasps. "What? How?" Her hand covers her mouth, shock ever present.

This is going to be so hard. I never told anyone about this, except for Sebastian and I haven't seen him since that day. Ugh. "When I was fifteen, I witnessed my father murder my mother."

"WHAT?!"

"FUCK!"

"No…"

All three spoke or shouted at once. I close my eyes to help contain my composure. "I heard them arguing in the bedroom. Mind you it wasn't the first time I heard them, but I was tired of it, so I was going to tell them to stop." I pause and look to Jack. He squeezes my hand and nods for me to go on. "Only when I opened the bedroom door and walked in, it was just in time to see my father stab my mother in chest." Tears started to leak down my face, I had no control over them. I blink trying to stop them, but it doesn't help.

Jack sets a box of tissues in my lap. I look up to him and smile a small smile for him. "Thanks." I take one and wipe my face. Clearing my throat, I continue. "My father heard me come in the room and looked up. His face was beet red, full of anger. He pulled the knife from my mother's chest and tossed it aside. I stood in shock for a moment, watching his every move until he stood. Then I tried to run." I shake my head. "I tripped and he caught up to me. He threw me against a wall, I broke my arm. I did get away, but it wasn't for long. I ran right into my father's driver. I thought for sure I was dead. But I was wrong. Sebastian saved me. He helped me get a new identity and leave the US. Since then, I've never looked back." I blow out a breath and watch each of their expressions, waiting for questions.

"That's a very big secret to carry alone." Gabe says while he holds a now grief stricken Belle. Tears run down her face as she looks at me.

"It's been my burden to carry." I tell him. "Belle? I'm still me. You just now know my alter ego." I try and giggle in an attempt to make her laugh with me. It doesn't work.

After a few minutes of awkward silence, Jack clears his throat and asks the question I'd hoped he forgot. "Are you going to tell me now why you have to leave the city?" He raises his eyebrows in question.

This catches Belle's attention. She sits up in her chair and wipes the tears from her face. "You're leaving?"

I give Belle a sad face and turn to Jack and scowl. I wanted to tell that part slowly, but apparently Jack's impatient. "Well, my father is a senator in Washington. He has many connections. When Jack had his friend do a search for me, I'm almost a hundred percent certain someone on my father's end would've been made aware of this." I take a slow, deep breath. "If he knows I'm alive he'll come for me. He'll finish what he started."

"Like fuck he will!" Jack grunted. "You're not going anywhere. You're staying here. We'll protect you." He narrows his eyes, lips thin and fierce. His anger is fully present. The way he looks at this moment, Jack's definitely not a man to reckon with.

I bow my head and close my eyes. I don't want anyone to get hurt. Why can't they see that?

CIRCUMSTANCES UNRAVELED

CHAPTER SEVENTEEN
Jack

My heart's pounding. My lungs constrict. Anger. I need to calm myself. I look to Mel and see that she's docile. Defeated. Tears leak from her face and land on the sheets in her lap. Suddenly, my anger's gone.

"Mel?" Belle calls from across the room. Mel shakes her head.

I look to Belle and she shrugs her shoulders. Gabe does the same.

I lean close to Mel and whisper. "Baby, are you okay?"

"I don't want you to get hurt, Jack. I don't want anyone to get hurt." She mumbles.

Ah, fuck it. I put the rail down on the bed and gently push Mel over. I sit beside her and pull her close, wrapping my arm around her. Her head falls to my shoulder and I start to caress her hair. "Oh, baby, we'll all be okay. Don't you worry about us. Gabe and I are trained for this shit and Belle will be with you." I kiss the top of her head and then hold her. "The local police are searching for Matt and Riley. Let us do this. Trust us."

She reaches her arm up and takes ahold of my hand. "Are you sure?"

"We got this. Nobody's going to hurt you. Ever! You are mine to protect. Mine to hold. Mine to love.

As long as you let me, Mel." I give her a gentle squeeze and hear her sigh in content.

"It's about time." Belle grumbles and Gabe chuckles from across the room. I look to them and smile. They must've known something was brewing between us before we did. Oh, well. Love is in the air and I can't deny it.

"So…do we have a plan?" Mel asks as she sits up and turns her head to look at me.

I gaze into her gorgeous eyes and stare for a moment. I see fear right off, but I also see trust. And damn, I'm the luckiest man around to have earned that. Trust is the hardest thing to gain and I know if I lose it, I may never get it back. I'll do my damnest to keep it. The longer I stare, I see her skin flush. I smile and glance to her lips. They look soft and very much inviting. Calling for me. Who am I to ignore an invitation? I look back up into her eyes and lean in. I gently place my lips on hers and fuck, I was right. Soft, warm and they taste like coffee. I want more, but I won't push. I run my tongue along the seam for an extra taste and nibble gently. She kisses me back and I'm in heaven. Why I ignored her courageous advances not so long ago, I don't know. I'm kicking myself now, that's for sure. After another taste I pull back and rest my forehead on hers.

There's a knock on the door, but no one walks in. Strange considering everyone else just walks in after they knock. "Come in." I shout.

In walks a tall, thin, blonde man, holding hands with a young blonde haired child. I watch as he closes the door and turns to look at all of us. His glance stops at Mel. "Oh, thank God I found you."

Mel stares at the man scrunching her nose and narrowing her eyes for a moment. Then her mouth opens in an 'O' shape and her eyes pop open. "Sebastian? Is that you?" She asks.

The man, I guess his name is Sebastian, nods. "Yes. And this is my little girl, Lilly. I hate to barge in on you, but I've driven over ten hours and asked anyone and everyone possible of your whereabouts."

The little girl moves closer to her father and wraps her arms around his legs. He puts his arm around her in reassurance, I assume.

"He knows, doesn't he?" Mel asks. Worry etches over her face.

With a grim expression, he nods. "Your only Godsend is your identity. He has no idea of the one you use now. I packed up and ran before he could get answers. I wanted to come warn you before I ran further from him. He already..." He drops his voice to a whisper. "Threaten to harm my daughter." He looks down at her and takes a breath. "This was after he admitted that he basically killed my wife not long ago. I can't do this anymore." He reaches in his pocket and pulls out a piece of paper. There's a number on it. He hands it to Mel. "This is a number I can be reached. It's a burner cell. Whenever you are ready, I can help you bring your father down. That's if you want to. For now, I need to get my daughter somewhere safe."

I interrupt the interaction between them. This is the man that helped my woman escape a murderous man. He gave her a new life. He gave me her. He needs help now. "Stay. Let us help you." I tell him. "You once gave a young girl a chance at life. Let us…" I wave my hand around the room. "Be there for you. Let us help you give you and your daughter a chance at life." I raise my eyebrows and wait.

Mel nods quickly in agreement. "Yes! I agree. Please, Sebastian. Our men have connections, too. They can help." I look to her and smile, proud to see her seeing things my way. Here I thought she gave up on running because we would've ganged up on her, but really? She did it for me. She honestly believes in me. Damn, that feels good.

Sebastian looks like he's pondering the idea. I know he doesn't know us. But if he's smart, he'll understand what's at stake here and that we're the good guys offering a helping hand. Sebastian blows out a breath and kneels down to his daughter. "Lilly, would you like to stay with my friends for a little while with me? It'll be like a vacation." He asks her softly. His daughter looks no older than five years old and she's cute as a button. I hope one day to have a few just as adorable.

She looks around the room slowly, shy as can be and back to her father. "Okay, daddy. I'm hungry." She says in her little voice and he chuckles.

"We'll get something to eat in a few minutes, sweetie." He stands up and looks to me. "It looks like we'll stick around. I guess we'll go grab something to eat and check into a hotel."

"Nonsense." Belle blurts out. We all turn to her in confusion. "You can stay at Mel's place and she can stay at Jack's. That way we all know who's where. Plus, it's cheaper for you, Sebastian." Belle smiles big and winks at me.

I laugh to myself. I see what Belles up to—sneaky woman that she is. But hell, I have no problems with having my woman with me, in my bed. I look to Mel to see if she has a problem with it.

She stares at me. Her eyes are bright, shining with mischief. Biting her lip then licking it. "I think it's manageable."

"Are you sure about this? We don't want to be a burden." Sebastian asks.

"No, no problem at all." I tell him with a big grin.

CIRCUMSTANCES UNRAVELED

CHAPTER EIGHTEEN
Mel

I give Sebastian the keys from my purse. Belle writes down my address and gives it to him. He and little Lilly leave to go get settled in. Jack tells him that he'll call him later to brief him on any plans that are made.

The nurse comes in just after everyone leaves—except Jack—and gives me something more for pain. All the talking made my jaw ache something fierce. Now I feel much better.

There's a knock on the door and my doctor comes in with a smile on his face and my chart in his hand. "Well, Mel, everything looks great. With the exception of that little seizure when you started to regain your memory, you're almost good as new." He flips through the chart, scribbles down something, and rips out a small sheet of paper. He hands it over to Jack. "This is a prescription for some pain meds. You take them when needed—and sparingly. They're strong and can be addicting. I shouldn't have to tell you that, being a nurse and all." He smirks. "You have the choice to stay another night, or if you'd like you can go home today, with the promise of returning if there are any problems at all. What do you think?"

I can go home, already? Well, hells bells. I look to Jack. He raises his eyebrows and smiles. I return his smile. "I think I'll go home if that's okay, Dr. Horsley." I look back at him. "Thank you for everything. I promise to return if there are any problems."

"Very well, Mel. Take care of yourself." He closes the chart and leaves.

Excitement courses through me at the prospect of leaving. I fling my legs over the side of the bed and get ready to stand, but Jack stops me.

"Slow down, firecracker. Let me help you." He grins and stands up. "What can I do for you?" He asks.

I think for a minute then smirk. "You can take that sexy ass over to the closet and get my bag so I can get dressed." I waggle my eyebrows at him and bite my lip.

He shakes his head. "And there she is. My firecracker is back." He leans down and places a hard kiss on my lips. Not hard enough to hurt, but hard enough to show that he means it. I accept his lips and push back, nipping and licking with hunger for him.

When he pulls back and turns, I smack his ass. "Get my bag, hot stuff." I giggle and he chuckles.

We walk into Jack's place and I look around. It's a decent size and modern looking. Jack bought the house after everything was settled with Belle's case. He said he was going to settle down in one place for a while and see how things go. Plant roots is what he told me at the coffee shop before everything happened. I'm glad he did, or I wouldn't be with him right now.

I walk further into the room and see that it's the living room. The walls are a dark grey and plain. Plush black furniture sit pushed against the walls. A television large in size sits in the center of the room. The floor is hardwood. Even though there are no pictures on the wall the room still looks decent. You can tell it's a man's room.

Jack walks past me with my bags and talks over his shoulder. "I'll put these in the bedroom. Be right back."

"Okay." I tell him as I keep wandering the house. Off to the left is the kitchen, with stainless steel appliances and light multi-color marble counter top. The floor again is hardwood. The room is spacious and gorgeous. This is a woman's room and I love it. There's a window above the sink, I move to it and look out. The scenery is beautiful, trees and flowers spread in the distance. I walk to the right and head down a hallway where I bump into Jack. "Hey."

"Checking things out?" He asks.

"Of course I am, silly." I step around him and continue on my journey. Jack follows me. I push open the door to the left to find a small bathroom with a pedestal white sink, a simple white toilet, and tub and shower combo. The walls are beige and the floors are a white tile of some kind. There's a small window with blinds on it, and a shelf over the toilet. The mirror over the sink is small, but all together the bathroom is quaint but doable.

Jack is leaning on the wall outside the room when I exit and he looks at me with amusement. I just step past him and move to the last room in the house. I enter and my mouth drops open. The room is amazing. In the center of the room is a king size bed with large plush pillows and a dark blue comforter. The walls match the bed being a dark blue. The floor is hardwood matching the rest. End tables sit on each side of the bed with a matching dresser against one wall and on the other wall is a large patio door with dark curtains, which are open. Definitely a man's room, but still I love it. And it smells just like Jack. I take a deep breath in and turn around. "Your house is gorgeous, Jack."

From where he leans in the door way, he walks toward me. "It looks even more gorgeous with you in it." He reaches me and wraps his arms around me.

I wrap my arms around him and look up into his eyes. "I need to admit something to you." I feel him tense a little. "Relax, it's not bad." I smile to reassure him.

He relaxes and gazes at me. "Tell me, baby. What's up?"

I reach a hand up and cup his cheek. Staring into his eyes I pray he sees the truth. "I've never felt safe. These past fifteen years, there's always been this fear that had me worried, that had me looking over my shoulder when I felt something was off. But with you, I feel safe." I caress his cheek and watch his face. I think over the feelings that have built for this man since we met. From the instant lust I felt when I first laid eyes on him to the comfort I had with being around him, enough that I was able to tease him and joke around.

To be in his house now? We've come so far, despite the obstacles.

Jack reaches up and puts his hand over mine on his face and leans down and places a soft, gentle kiss on my lips. I feel the truth there. He hears me. He believes me. "Thank you." He reaches down wrapping an arm under my knees and wrapping an arm around my shoulders, picking me up. I let out a little yelp and giggle. He moves to set me on the bed.

I move up on the bed so my head is on the pillow and watch him. "What are you doing all the way over there?" I ask him as he stands at the end of the bed. I smirk at him. Teasing a little never hurt anyone. Even though I'm a bit apprehensive about how I'll react to being touched after what Matt and Riley did to me, I can't let fear control me. I have strong feelings for Jack and I want to show him. It's taken me a long time to get where I am in this life—finally finding a good man. I feel I deserve Jack and I'll have him—if he'll take me.

He looks me over and heat flashes in his eyes. I know he feels it, too. He blinks and shakes his head. "Do you need anything for pain?"

Seriously? I'm throwing the hints and he knows it, but maybe he's right. I did just get released from the hospital. I should take a night and get my bearings. That doesn't mean we can't lie together and hold each other. Just being held would be a good start for healing, at least I think so. "No, Jack. I'm good. Please, come here." I shake my head and bite my bottom lip right after.

CIRCUMSTANCES UNRAVELED

The heat reappears in his eyes immediately.

CHAPTER NINETEEN
Jack

Stupid, stupid, stupid...what am I thinking? Take the damn invite man. She's calling me out. Isn't she? I stare her down, looking her body over. Fuck, she has a hot body. I can't wait to see it naked. I want to taste every part of her.

I kick my shoes off and get on the bed.

"Wait." She whispers as she rolls to her side, reaching a hand toward me, asking, encouraging me to spoon with her. "Can you just hold me? I know I might be sending mixed signals and I'm sorry, but I'd like to be just held for tonight. Please." She looks over her shoulder at me with sincere eyes.

I wiggle the blankets out from under her and pull them up and over us. I tuck my body tight behind her and wrap my arm around her waist. If she wants to cuddle, I'll cuddle the crap right out of her. I'll give her anything she asks. After what she has been through, she deserves it.

She takes my hand and wraps her fingers with mine and sighs in content. I smile to myself, happy that I make her feel this way.

"Sleep, baby. If you need anything, just ask." I kiss the back of her head, breathing in her scent. I close my eyes and relax.

I wake to a restless Mel. She's mumbling and kicking her legs. A nightmare maybe? I gently shake her, trying to wake her when she screams herself awake.

"Shhh, baby. I got you. It's just a dream." I try to calm her down.

Her breathing is labored and sweat edges her forehead. I still don't know all the details of her time in captivity, but I can just imagine what she went through. I brush her hair off her face and wait for her to respond.

"I'm sorry to wake you, Jack. It was awful. The things they did…" She closes her eyes and swallows deeply. "It makes me feel so…" She whispers.

"I'm sorry you had to go through that, Mel. But you're safe now. What can I do to help?" I rub her arm as she turns over to her back in the bed.

She looks at me in the eyes, her eyes glisten with unshed tears. "Make love to me. Erase the evil they left behind. Please." She pleads.

I toss the blankets aside and move to the end of the bed. I watch her eyes with my every move. Her skin goes flush, pink—and I haven't even touched her. I feel my dick getting hard, twitching with need. I crawl up the bed, moving over her slender body, pushing her shirt up, and kissing her stomach along the way. I hear her breath catch with each kiss and it spurs me on. I breathe her in and her smell is intoxicating. She smells like fresh peaches and I love it.

I push her shirt up further and she sits up enough for me to push it right up and over her head. I toss it on the floor and drift my eyes back to her now shirtless torso. A simple pink lace bra now covers her breasts. I dip my face down and nuzzle the smooth area between her boobs. I lick and nibble my way from one to the other as I reach around and unclasp her bra. Slowly I pull down the straps and pull away the piece of clothing obstructing me from my target. I peek up at Mel and see her smile. Her eyes sparkle and are full of heat. Lust.

I take a nipple into my mouth and suck leisurely, as I fondle the other until it peaks. I release the one from my mouth with a wet pop and move to the other to give it equal attention. Mel's hand grips my hair and I hear her moan. My cock presses against my zipper. It's hard and raring to go.

"Oh, Jack. That feels so good." Mel moans as she runs her fingers through my hair and presses her chest in my face.

I growl like an animal in horny excitement. I release my grip from her breast and lick my way down her stomach. Popping the button to her jeans, I rip the zipper apart and pull her pants down. I lean back on my knees, Mel having to let go of me and pull my shirt up and over my head. I throw it to the floor and stand at the end of the bed.

"I want you so much, Mel." I growl. I rip her pants and panties off and toss them aside. I'm quick with my own pants, stepping on them once they are down and kicking them away. I stand there for a moment, my gaze drifting over her naked body. I take her all in. "Fuck me. You are fucking gorgeous, baby."

117

I crawl up her body, caressing her legs, licking, kissing, nipping, until I reach her sweet pussy.

I hear her breath catch. I look up, panting. I want to eat her up. I want to take everything, every part of her and make her mine. Her eyes shine and sparkle. Lust. The heat and want shine back ten-fold, yelling at me 'yes'. That is all I need. I dive in, mouth first.

I lick her wet slit with my tongue and groan from her sweet taste. With my fingers, I spread her lips apart to get closer. I find her clit and latch on. I gently suck while I slide my finger up and down her pussy and when she moans, I slip my finger in.

"Jack..."

I pull my finger out and glide it up and down a few times then push two fingers in. I feel her pussy clamp down on me in little flutters as Mel begins to move her hips to my rhythm.

"You taste fucking amazing, baby. I can't get enough." I say between sucks. I pump my fingers faster and harder, watching her body enjoy the pleasure she's receiving. For the hell of it (and to give her more pleasure) I slip in a third finger and listen to her groan. She's tight, but I make it work.

"Oh, my God! Jack! Don't stop. Please. Harder." She mumbles between gasping breaths.

I speed up the thrusts of my fingers and lick around her clit some more. I feel her tight pussy starting to spasm and her hip action becomes irregular. She's going to come. "That's it, baby. Come for me." I tell her and suck hard on her clit.

Mel comes hard on my tongue and fingers. Her body spasms and vibrates. Her skin flushes. It's the most beautiful thing I've seen. I remove my fingers and lick them clean. Kissing my way up her body, I make my way to her mouth. I slip my tongue between her luscious lips and start a tango. A battle, if you will. I lick her tongue, her lips and she does the same. The battle doesn't last long. My dick needs relief.

"I need inside of you, baby. And I mean now."

"Yes. Yes. Yes." She puffs out, all out of breath.

I reach over to my night stand and pull out a condom from the drawer. I lean back, rip open the package and slide the sucker on. I lean back down over Mel and kiss her passionately. I feel her pussy with my cock so I move my hips a little to slide it up and down, getting it a little wet before I start to push in.

With the tip just at the entrance, I gaze into Mel's eyes. I let all my emotions show in my one look. I know during sex isn't the time to say it, but I fucking love this woman. I just hope I get the chance to prove it to her. I lean down and press a soft kiss to her lips and slowly thrust my hard cock in her wet pussy.

She moans and I groan.

"Fuck!"

"Jesus Christ, you feel so damn good." I say. I stay still once I'm all the way in and take a deep breath. Slowly I pull back and press back in and groan again. I feel a shiver run through Mel's body. She reaches her hands around me and grabs my ass.

"More. I want more, Jack."

Jesus fuck. This woman will kill me. I'm trying not to be a teenager and blow after three strokes and she's asking for the world. Fuck me. I calm myself and pull back a bit and press forward again. Three slow breaths and I think I have it under control.

I pull almost all the way out and slam back in hard. Fuck that felt good. I do it again. Yes! Again. Faster. Harder.

"Yes, Jack. Again." She moans as she lifts her hips to meet mine. She squeezes my ass and pulls me in.

I thrust again and again. Sweat begins to pool between our bodies, but I don't care. Mel feels to damn good to worry about shit like that. I lean toward her and take her mouth with mine. I tangle my tongue with hers and start a passionate battle of wills while I thrust hard and long, taking and giving everything I have, marking her, making her mine.

I feel her pussy clamp hard around my cock and my balls begin to tingle. We're both ready to blow. "Come for me, baby. Give me everything you have." I tell her.

She clenches her eyes shut and her body starts to tremble. I thrust my cock in her gorgeous body two more times and shout my release. "Mel…"

"Jack…"

We both finish and I kiss her softly, pull out, and roll to the side leaning on my elbow. I watch her, her beautiful naked body still on display for me.

"I will protect you with my life, baby." I promise her. "Nothing will ever hurt you again. You're mine."

CHAPTER TWENTY
Mel

It's been a few days since Jack and I made love. It was amazing and I want more of it, but he's been busy working with Gabe on my case or should I say cases. The men who kidnapped me and raped me, Matt and Riley are still on the loose. I shiver with the thought. With the knowledge that my father knows I'm alive, we need to build a case big enough to shut him down. Jack and Gabe have been doing research, getting names and other things that they think will help with what Sebastian and I know.

I haven't left Jack's house since I arrived here. Belle has been here on and off over the past few days, but she has to work. I'm not ready to return to work. Eventually I will, but just not yet.

Sebastian and his little girl, Lilly are coming over this afternoon to talk to me and Jack. He says he has some stuff that'll help with the case. Stuff he never told anyone about.

Right now, I'm attempting to make an ice coffee with Jack's Keurig machine, but it's not going very well. I'm making a mess and I'm ready to say fuck it and just have hot chocolate.

My jaw feels much better. I have only taken one pill today which is awesome considering what I've been through. All my cuts are healed and the bruises are all gone. I'm back to myself and I feel good about it.

I give up on the ice coffee, clean up my mess and make hot chocolate. At least there's some caffeine in it. I head to the living room and sit in the comfy couch. I made Jack order Netflix since he was going to be working, I need something to do while he's gone. I flick through the movies and television shows and decide on watching a movie. One of my favorites is on, so I pick it. Step up.

I'm snuggled up with a blanket when my new cell phone rings. Belle got me a new one. She knew I'd be lost without it. I look to the phone and see it's an unknown number. I ignore it. A few minutes later my cell beeps with a text message. I look at it and it shows one new message. Of course, curiosity wins and I open it to see what it says.

My heart pounds out of my chest (or at least it feels like it) and my breath is sucked right out of my lungs…well, it feels like it.

How is my lovely daughter doing on this fine, Canadian day?

Shit! He's here. He's found me. I jump from the couch and start pacing the room. What do I do? I rush to the door and make sure it's locked. It is. I check each room to make sure all the windows are locked, they are. Immediately I dial Jack's number and put the phone to my ear.

He answers on the first ring. "What's wrong, Mel?"

"He's here. He's found me, Jack. He called. Well, he texted. But I think he tried calling. Fuck. Where are you?" I'm freaking the fuck out. I need him here. I need to feel safe before I lose my ever-loving mind.

"Lock everything. I'll be there in twenty."

The call ends and I continue to pace the room. My nerves are a wreck. I knew my father had connections, but I didn't think he'd find me this fast. My phone beeps again and I jump. I open the message and a shiver runs up my spine.

I will see you soon, daughter of mine.

I toss my phone on the kitchen counter and go back to the couch. I lean over the back of it and peek out the window, watching, making sure no one is out there. I pray Jack hurries home.

I stare at the clock on the wall, impatiently as my anxiety rises and it feels as if the time hasn't moved at all. Where the fuck is Jack? I'm ready to pull my hair out, I'm so freaked out. What if my father gets me first?

The front door whips open and I scream.

"Jesus Christ, baby, it's just me." Jack says as he shuts the door and locks it again. I didn't even hear the door unlock, that is how paranoid I was. He rushes to my side and pulls me in for a hug. He holds me tight. "Everything will be okay. I'm here now. Shh…."

My body trembles even though my safe hold is gripping me tight. "He's coming for me, Jack." I shiver.

He brushes his hand through my hair. "You need to relax, Mel. He'll have to go through me first."

I pull back and look at him. Is he serious? "You can't get hurt, Jack. I don't want you getting hurt. I told you that." I start pacing the room.

I'm in the hall when Jack crushes his body up against mine. He grabs my hands and puts them up over my head. He slowly backs me up against the wall, leaning in he whispers in my ear. "I told you to relax, baby. I plan to make your mind clear of all bad things, and make your body melt with my touch. At this time, it's just you and me in the world." He looks down and pierces my soul with his eyes. I see nothing but lust. He's in complete control. I feel myself begin to relax. He glides one hand down my arm, caressing the side of my breast, across my stomach and stops when he reaches the waist of my yoga pants. My breath hitches, and his eyes blaze. He leans in and gives me an earth-shattering kiss. I'm drunk in lust as he pulls away from me. Jack slides his hand down the front of my pants and finds my now wet pussy. I don't dare move an inch. I'm entranced, fearing that if I move he'll stop. I feel his fingers glide into my pussy and almost lose my footing. I have this insatiable need for Jack to fulfil, and he's fulfilling the need completely. "Are you beginning to relax, baby?" He asks me in a hushed tone, barely above a whisper.

"Uh huh." I mumble with a breathy voice.

"Good girl." As he continues to finger my wet greedy pussy, he presses his thumb to my clit. With just the right amount of pressure, he rubs my sensitive nub in circles. My release builds up. His rhythm picks up and I start to grind my hips. It feels amazing. As I drop my head against the wall, my impending orgasm looms. My head starts getting fuzzy from the sensations I feel.

"Oh, fuck yes, mmm, Jack. Yes! I'm coming." I let out a guttural groan as I feel my pussy clamp down around his fingers.

"Beautiful. Just fucking gorgeous." He whispers.

I relax and open my eyes. He pulls his hand from my pants and sucks my juices from his fingers. "Feel better now, baby?" He smirks.

I blow out a breath and smile. "Yes. Thank you. Sorry for freaking out. It's just I've never been afraid of anything or anyone as much as I am of him." He wraps his arm around my shoulder and guides me back to the living room. He has me sit on the couch.

"Where's your phone?" He asks.

I point toward the kitchen. "On the counter."

He goes and grabs it and comes and sits beside me. I read the text messages because I hadn't been able to tell him about the second one yet and Jack looks to me. "I told Gabe and Sebastian to meet us in an hour. We need to get things moving."

I snuggle into his warm body and sigh. "I know. I just hope we can do what we set out to do. I hope we have enough."

He kisses the top of my head and hugs me. "We will make do. We will make do."

CIRCUMSTANCES UNRAVELED

CHAPTER TWENTY - ONE
Jack

I get Mel to settle as she snuggles beside me and starts to fall asleep. The thought that her father terrifies her to the point of extreme anxiety upsets me. I run my fingers through her hair, gently stroking her soft lengths until her breathing evens out. With Mel finally sleeping I start to run scenarios through my mind of possibilities to fix the shit-storm that's become our lives.

I never thought I'd fall in love, not once in my thirty-five years…but I have and with a brave, beautiful woman with a sassy mouth to boot. I've learned that you can't control circumstances in life, but as Mel and I get closer I realize that even though everything that's happened was brutal, it took all of it to bring us together. It took us almost losing it all to bring out the truth from her past and for us to realize our feelings, our connection.

With everything Mel has gone through, the kidnapping and her past, I'm amazed with her strength. She accepts me, my touch, the intimacy we share and not even a flinch. She accepts me as a whole, understanding I'd never harm her. This I'm proud of, considering what she's gone through.

I can't wait to get a hold of those men. Matt and Riley. They sure are smarter than they look. Dex said that the CSIS has their photos out at all transportation outlets, including bus stations, trains, and planes. I made sure to mention that all border crossings are covered as well. There's no way we were letting these men get away. They'll pay for what they did to my sweet firecracker.

There's a knock on the door and I look to the clock. It's been just under an hour. Well, shit. I was spaced out in my own thoughts for quite some time. I look down and see Mel's still asleep. I slowly ease myself out from under her and get up to answer the door, leaving Mel leaning against the back of the couch. I unlock the door and slowly open it while shushing the people as they come in.

One by one Gabe, Belle, Sebastian, and little Lilly all walk in.

Gabe carries a laptop bag. Belle carries a tray of drinks. Lilly carries a bag that looks like it's full of toys and Sebastian has box full of...I don't really know. I guess I'll find out. They all head for my dining table and set things down—except Lilly. She hides behind her father, clutching his leg, shy as can be.

"Lilly, sweetie, you can play in the living room over here if you like." I tell her and walk over to where Mel still sleeps.

Lilly peeks around her father's legs and up at him. "Can I?" She asks him in a sweet small voice.

He smiles down at her. "You sure can. Go on over."

Lilly takes her bag of toys and heads over and sits on the floor in front of the television. She opens her bag and starts pulling out a bunch of toys. I have no idea what's what, but I'm happy she can play.

I go to the couch and gently shake Mel's shoulder. "Mel, baby, wake up. Everyone's here." I watch as her eyes slowly flutter open and I smile at her.

"Oh, hey. I fell asleep. Sorry." She yawns as she covers her mouth. Opening her eyes more she sees why she was woken. "Shit. Sorry. Hey, everyone." She immediately stands up and looks around, noticing Lilly. "Sorry, Sebastian."

Sebastian chuckles. "It's okay, it's not the first time she's heard that word."

We all gather around the table and Belle hands out drinks to each of us.

Sebastian opens his box and sets the lid on the floor. "I mentioned that I might have some stuff that will help fight the senator." He starts pulling file folders out of the box and setting them on the table. The blonde man before me (who looks older than his thirty-six years) must've been collecting shit on the senator for many years by the looks of it. I watch as he piles folder after folder on the table. "I've labeled the folders by year."

"Holy sh—smokes, Sebastian. This is all on my father?" Mel asks with wide eyes as she picks up a file and opens it.

I continue to watch the folders pile up until he empties the box and sets it on the floor with the lid. He sits in the chair and looks around the table. "So, this is what I have. Let's see what we can use."

Mel and Belle's jaws both drop. Gabe looks at the man and then to me. I just shake my head. "Alright, let's do this." I sit in a chair and we all start to root through the files.

We've been through about a quarter of the files and so far we have found some pretty damaging information. Fraud, embezzlement and cover up for little unknown schemes. Belle lets out a gasp and covers her mouth. "Oh, my god." She stares at the file she is looking at and looks to Mel.

Mel and everyone else looks to Belle. "What is it?" Mel asks as she closes the file she has in her hands, scrunching her nose and narrowing her eyes, concern ever present.

"Your mom." Is all Belle says and Mel grabs the file from her, immediately looking down on the papers. There in plain sight are all the documents that Sebastian kept about the cover up he did for the senator after he murdered her mother.

Mel looks to Sebastian. "You kept documents on everything? There are even pictures here, Sebastian." She swallows. "What made you do that?"

Sebastian sets the file down that he was holding and folds his hands together. "Honestly, after you told me what you saw and what he did to you, I didn't trust him. And after he threatened my family, there was no way I was doing my job without having a back-up plan." He looks over his shoulder at his little girl and back. "I have too much to live for now and I owe it to you to make him pay. I hope it helps." He picks up the folder he was looking through and opens it again.

"Bingo!" Gabe pipes up. We all turn to him. "Here's the file about her supposed death." *Shit that's two things we have strong against him. Things are looking up.* "Sebastian, man, you keep great records." Gabe smacks him on the back and continues to root through the folders.

A cell phone pings informing us that a message is waiting. Everyone checks. It's Mel's. Her facial expression begins to scare me.

Are you working today, dear daughter? Turn on your television.

CIRCUMSTANCES UNRAVELED

CHAPTER TWENTY - TWO
Mel

I read the text over and wonder what the hell he's talking about. I look to the television and know that I can't turn it on with Lilly there so I hand my phone to Jack.

"What the fuck?" He gets up and grabs his laptop from the living room, bringing it back to the table and powering it on. He loads it to the local news network and swears. "Fuck!"

There on the screen playing live says it all. A shiver runs down my spine. I pull my knees up and hug them to my chest.

Local Hospital on Lockdown and Isolated Due to Bomb Threat. City Police on the scene.

Jack reaches over and touches my shoulder. "He won't get you. We won't let him." He tells me, but I can tell he holds back. He's angry and why wouldn't he be? I'm angry, but I'm scared too. My father's playing games, messing with my head. Why can't he just fuck off already?

I take a deep breath and close my eyes. I've let my fear run my life for far too long when it comes to my father. I now have friends that I consider family and documented proof of his evil doings. It's time I take back my life and stand up to the man who thinks he can control everyone. I open my eyes and look at Jack.

"I know. He won't get me, I won't let him. I'm done running, Jack." I look around the table to everyone, and back to Jack. "Call Dex and let's get this bastard. I'm not afraid of him anymore." Well, I sort of am, but I'm not backing down. I want a life with Jack, with my friends. I need to do this.

Jack stands from the table nodding. "I'm on it." He walks down the hall and out of view.

I drop my legs to the floor. "Anyone hungry?" I ask as I stand and head to the kitchen.

"Me." Lilly yells from the living room. We all laugh. I open the freezer door and search the contents to see what's available to cook. I find a couple pounds of hamburger. Taking it out, I set it on the counter and open the cupboard doors in search of something to mix with meat. Spaghetti sauce, perfect.

"Spaghetti sound good?" I call over my shoulder to everyone.

A resounding 'yes' is returned from everyone. I smile and get to making some food. Keeping myself occupied is what I need right now, either that or my mind would be wandering to places I don't need it to be.

It's evening now. Sebastian has left with Lilly and has promised to be available if need be. Dinner went over well, lots of laughter and smiles to keep the night light for Lilly. We want to keep Lilly out of the situation as much as we can. Jack and Gabe are in the living room watching something on the television and I

134

just got out of the shower. Heading to the bedroom, I find Belle sitting on the bed, waiting.

"Hey, you. Feel better?" Belle asks as she pats a spot on the bed beside her.

I secure the towel around me and sit on the bed, turning toward her. "Shower felt great, but no, my nerves are still shot."

Belle leans over and wraps her arms around me. "The guys will make sure everything works out."

I return the hug. "I know." I tell her with a small smile. Thinking about everything that has been talked about recently, I feel bad for holding everything in. Belle has been my best friend for years, why I never confided in her I don't really know. And now she's stuck in this shit storm of mine. Well, I never wanted this to ever happen. "Sorry about all this." I whisper.

Belle pulls back and looks me right in the eye. "Enough. This isn't your fault. Sure, you kept your true identity from me. I don't understand why, but you didn't ask for all this to happen. I don't blame you for anything. I love you, Mel. I'll always be here for you. You're my best friend. Never forget that."

Wow. What a kick to the chest that is. It hurts to feel the truth, but it also feels good to know that she's always there. "I love you too, hon." I tell her as I wipe the lonely tear that escapes and starts down my cheek.

"Okay, enough with the hard stuff. How are things with you and Jack?" Belle asks with huge smile on her face.

Feeling heat cover my face, I know I'm blushing. I bite my lip and smile. "Things are great."

Belle pulls her leg up onto the bed and tucks it under her bottom. "Really? That's all I get?" Eagerness and happiness flowing through her body language as she bounces on the bed.

I laugh and shake my head at her silliness. "Okay, fine. Things are better than great. Jack's fucking amazing. Is that better?" I say as I stick my tongue out at her. I pull my legs up on the bed and get comfortable. But seriously, although I was super nervous deep down before, for the first time in my life things feel right. I want Jack's touch more than I wanted anything else before. I feel love with every kiss, every caress. The way he looks at me. He'll help me heal. He already is." I haven't had girl talk in so long. It feels good to leave the rest of the world outside of these walls and just be us girls. "What about you and Gabe?" I raise my eyebrows.

"Well..." She looks over to see that the door is still shut and turns back to me. "...when Gabe brought me to his place all those months ago, after my surgery, he showed me his room." I nod my head to show her I am listening. "At that time, I was a bit shy, you remember with everything going on."

"Yes, I do. Not a time I want to relive." I frown. "But anyways, go on." I tell her.

"In his room, I found some intriguing things." She smirks.

I bite my lip and raise my eyebrows. "Do tell."

Her cheeks start to pink as she speaks. "Hand cuffs, lubricant, a cock ring and vibrators." She bites her lip and her blushed cheeks get darker.

136

I'm shocked to hear this. I remember hearing the men mentioning something about control a while back, and I have of course read many of books that discuss kinky things, but never once did it cross my mind that Gabe was a kinky man. "Wow. So, do you and Gabe do the whole kinky sex play thing? You know, like in the books?" My interest is thoroughly peeked.

She nods quickly and whispers. "Yes."

I start to bounce on the bed, excited for my friend. "That's awesome. Do you like it? Are you not scared or nervous?" I need to know. When I read about it, it sounds amazing, so one can never know for sure.

"It took me some time to get the nerve to agree to play time, but oh my God, YES. It's worth it. The best orgasms I've ever had." Belle gushes as she looks to the door again, afraid that someone might come in.

I look to the door too, out of habit. "I'm so happy for you." I take a hand of hers and squeeze it. "I hope one day I can be brave and talk to Jack about that stuff. By the way Gabe and Jack talk, I'm sure Jack would be up for it." I smirk.

Belle nods in agreement. "I think he is."

"Belle, let's go, babe." We hear Gabe yell from the living room.

"Awe. Well, we'll have to have girl time again soon."

"For sure." I tell her as we get up from the bed and head out of the room.

CIRCUMSTANCES UNRAVELED

CHAPTER TWENTY – THREE
Jack

I watch as Gabe and Belle pull out of the driveway. Locking the door, I turn off the lights and head to the bedroom. I find Mel bent over digging through her bag, probably for some clean clothes. I sneak up behind her and place my hands on her hips.

Mel gasps. I smile.

She's only wearing a towel, wrapped snuggly around her slender body. Her long, dark tresses hang over her shoulders. I push them aside so I can kiss her shoulder. I press my lips to her exposed skin, smelling her. Cocoa butter—such a wonderful smell coming from her soft skin. I nip at her shoulder moving up to her neck, sucking until I reach her ear. I whisper. "You're the most beautiful woman I've ever seen."

Mel stands up straight and slowly turns herself in my arms. Pushing her hair over her shoulders, she looks up at me. "Am I now? Prove it." She stares into my eyes, watching me, waiting for my next move.

I raise my lips in a lazy smile. I accept her challenge. Moving my hands from her hips, I grip the ends of the towel, release its hold on her and allow it to fall to the floor. There she stands, gloriously naked before me. I lean down and press my lips to her pink lips in a hard kiss.

I scoop her up into my arms and walk over to the bed and set her on it.

I take a moment to take in her beauty, trying to believe that she's really here, that she's really mine, then I'm quick to strip myself of my clothes.

I lay on the bed beside Mel, leaning on my elbow. I face her so I can watch her reaction to my touch. I want to see her. I need her to know that I want to see her, to know that I want her and only her. I reach a hand over and brush her hair out of her face, caressing her cheek, down around her chin. Leaning toward her I kiss her forehead lightly, whisper touches with my lips to her eyes, her nose, her cheeks, her chin, and finally her mouth. I press harder, opening my mouth taking her bottom lip in and sucking lightly, nibbling.

Her breathing increases as she opens for me. I slip my tongue in and press further. I take control letting the passion between us sear our mouths together in bliss. I move my mouth down her neck, around to her ear and nibble lightly. Caressing her arm with my hand, up and down, around to her breast until I find a nipple. Working my way down, I lick, nip, and suck. I take the other nipple in my mouth and roll my tongue around it, sucking while my fingers work the other to a hard peek. I switch breasts as I look up at her.

Her eyes sparkle with lust as her chest heaves, starving for breaths. "Do you believe me now?" I taunt.

She licks her dry, pink lips and pants. "Almost." She grips the blankets with her small hands and I continue.

I glide my hand down her soft skin, down her stomach, until I reach the warmth between her legs. Mel moans to my touch. I move my body down on the bed and lick right above her mound, leaving a little wet area. I blow my warm breath over it and watch goose bumps rise. I love how she reacts to me. I slip my hand between her legs and she's wet. Fuck. "Wet already, firecracker. I love that." I swipe my fingers up and down a few times before I press a finger in her warm pussy.

"Jack…" She moans.

I use my thumb to search out her most sensitive area and press. Her clit is swollen and my teasing has already gotten her far. I know it won't take long. I circle my thumb around the nub and press harder. I insert a second finger and thrust fast, listening to the sounds she makes. Her smell drives me crazy. My cock is demanding relief. I don't think I'll be able to tease for much longer.

I feel her pussy clamp around my fingers. Mel's breathing is rapid. Her hips have started to move to the same rhythm as my hand. I move faster. Harder. "Do you believe me now?" I ask as I breathe harder, trying to control myself. I need inside her so fucking bad.

I feel her body start to shake. Her pussy grips my fingers tight and she screams. "Yes, Jack. Yes. I believe you."

"Thank fuck!" I yell and I thrust my fingers in and out until she finishes coming. I pull them out, stick my fingers in my mouth and groan. So, fucking good. I pull Mel over me so she straddles me and smile at her.

"Never forget that. You're beautiful." I look into her eyes as I hold her. I don't know if or when it'll ever be the best time to tell a woman about your feelings, but I don't give a shit anymore. What I feel for this woman, is everything and I need to tell her. "One other thing. I love you, Mel." I lean up and press my warm lips to hers giving her everything I have in that one kiss.

She takes me and gives back. She lifts herself so I take the opportunity to line my cock up with her damp pussy and she slowly slides down on me. I groan.

"I love you too, Jack. I have even before I knew who I was. I was just afraid to say anything." She takes all of me and grinds her pelvis against me. And fuck doesn't it feel amazing. Rising up, she drops back down setting a rhythm.

I grip her hips and help set the pace. I move faster, and harder, meeting her beat for beat. "Never be afraid of me, firecracker—never. I'll do everything in my power to keep you safe." I thrust up as she slams down. Fuck, I won't last. It feels too damn good. Up, down, grind. Up, down, grind. Fuck. "Baby, I'm gonna come."

Mel speeds up her pace. She must be close, too. I meet her pace as I feel her pussy clamp down on me. We both scream out as we release.

"Jack."

"Mel."

She falls down on me, sated. When we finish I roll her to the side so we can cuddle. My beautiful, strong, sassy, firecracker means the world to me. I don't care that she has a past. I know she has obstacles to get through, but I'll get her through them. I'll be by her side through it all. Once I thought I'd always be a bachelor, but now I'm a one-woman man. I'm Mel's man. Forever. Starting tomorrow, we flush all the shit down the toilet and start fresh. Move forward. Mel deserves that. I'll give her what she deserves.

CIRCUMSTANCES UNRAVELED

CHAPTER TWENTY - FOUR
Mel

I wake with my head resting on Jack's naked chest. His arms wrap around me, our legs tangle together—and it's the best thing I've experienced in my life so far. I breathe him in. His smell is intoxicating. He's every girl's wet dream. I lift the blanket that sits just above our waists, sneak a peek, and smile. Perfect—and he's all mine. I feel his breathing change. I think he is awake so I tip my head and look up at him.

Jack's smirking, he knows he caught me. "Looking for something?" He asks.

I giggle. Busted. "Can a girl not look? I thought I was dreaming, so I had to check." I suck at lying, but fuck I have to say something.

Jack shakes his head and grins, squeezing me tight (but not to hurt) he tips his head down and kisses my forehead. "Not a dream, baby. It's all me." He waggles his eyebrows and I don't know what he's going to do. Suddenly, he whips the blankets off of me and I shriek.

"Jack, what are you doing?" I laugh, scrambling for the blankets, but it's of no use. They're on the floor now.

Jack untangles his body from mine and lazily moves his eyes up and down my body. "Fair's fair, baby. You looked, now it's my turn."

I suppose he's right. I turn and hop off the bed. I stand beside the bed and slowly turn in a circle. "You like?" I ask as move slowly around, lifting my hair and letting fall over my naked breasts.

Jack growls and starts to crawl toward me from the bed.

I giggle because I know I'm teasing him. Being around Jack I feel that I can be me again—the woman who jokes around and plays. So that's what I'm doing. I'm being the woman I want to be, the woman who I'm meant to be. "Stop." I tell Jack before he pounces. "Play time later. Now we need to get dressed, eat, and head to Gabe's. Isn't Dex meeting us all somewhere this morning?" I raise my eyebrows in question.

"Shit." He frowns, looking sad like a lost puppy. Oh, my poor man. I'll make it up to him later. Right now we have things to deal with. "You're right." He gets up from the bed and walks toward the dresser. Along his way, he smacks my ass. "Get in the shower. I don't want to make everyone jealous."

I wrinkle my nose in confusion. "Jealous? How?"

"You smell like sex, baby. Poor Dex might get jealous—and jealous Dex makes for poor working conditions." He winks and smacks my ass again. "Get moving."

I laugh and head to the bathroom. "Okay, Mr. Bossy pants. But if I have to shower you do, too." I call over my shoulder.

We get to Gabe and Belles just before noon. Jack called Dex just before we left his place and told him to meet us there. Sebastian left the box of evidence at Jack's so I grabbed it before we left to bring with us. Jack pulls up in front of Gabe's place and parks. He reaches over to his glove compartment and pulls out a gun. I'm shocked to find that he has one. He tucks it in the back of his dark wash jeans and gets out of the truck. Walking around the vehicle, he opens my door and waits for me to exit. I bite my lip, thinking if I should ask him about the gun. I know his job's dangerous at times. He has connections with government agencies, so why wouldn't he have a gun? I shake my thoughts and step away from the truck. "Can you grab the box?" I ask him.

"No problem." He says, reaching in and grabbing it from behind my seat. He turns, shuts my door, and follows me in.

Gabe greets us at the door and takes the box from Jack. "Dex's already here. Come on in." Gabe tells us.

I remove my shoes and head over to the couch where Belle sits. I set my purse on the table and sit beside her. "Hey."

"Hey, you. Sleep well?" She asks.

I nod and smirk. Belle laughs. Just as I get comfortable my cell beeps from inside my bag. I reach for it and instantly the hairs on my neck stand up. I look around the room and a chill runs down my spine. "Where are Sebastian and Lilly?" I stutter in fear.

Everyone looks to me, I don't stutter, ever. So, when I do, everyone's attention is on me.

"On their way. What does the phone say, Mel?" Gabe asks, his tone very stiff but full of concern.

I look at my phone again, take a breath and read it. *Lilly looks just like her father. Would be a shame if something happened to her on this beautiful day.*

I read the message as clearly as I can. My emotions are getting the best of me, as usual. I look to Jack who's already moving toward me. He leans down and touches my shoulder. "Breathe, baby." He takes my phone and gives it to Dex. The pair of them sit at the table with laptops open and start doing all the techy crap that we know nothing about.

I hear Gabe talking, but I don't know to who. Then I hear Sebastian's name. I blow out a breath and a weight lifts. Gabe is talking to him on the phone. Apparently, I didn't hear it ring a moment ago. "He just pulled up. He and Lilly are fine." He goes to the door and heads down to let them in.

When they make it up the stairs and come inside, I rush to them and give Sebastian a hug. The look he gives is shock, but who blames him. He doesn't know what's going on. Next I lean down and give little Lilly a hug. She hugs me back and smiles. Lilly takes her bag and heads over to Belle who's waiting with arms wide open for a hug, too. Then she sits and opens her bag of toys to play.

I need a minute to myself so I head to the bathroom. I close the door and lean on the vanity. Closing my eyes, I start taking slow deep breaths. Why does life have to be so complicated? People need to leave sleeping bears lie. I hadn't thought of my father in years and now because of two assholes who wanted revenge on me, my past also wants revenge. I hate this. Just when I find love, I put it (and the man that means the world to me) to the ultimate test—to survive the wrath of revenge. I keep my tears at bay, blinking several times. I face the mirror, turn the water on, and lean down, splashing some water on my face to calm my nerves.

I hear a commotion in the living room. I wipe my face dry, open the door and head down the hallway. In the living room, everyone is surrounding the table, faces are red and everyone is arguing. "She can't do that." Belle shouts.

"It might be the only way." Dex returns.

"I won't ask her to do it." Jack says.

I have no idea of what's going on. I pass sweet little Lilly who's playing with her toys still, ignoring the adults and press my way into the mess of people. "What's going on?" I shout.

Everyone stops talking and looks at me. Jack moves to me and wraps his arms around me. I push him off of me. "NO, why's everyone arguing?"

Jack looks to everyone then back to me. "There was another text." He grimaces.

"And?"

Jack blows out a breath and reaches for my hand. I allow him to take it. "Your father wants to meet with you." He squeezes my hand gently and watches me, gazing into my eyes waiting.

I think about it for minute. If I meet with him he will kill me, but if we plan it right we can arrange it as a set up and bust him. Then again there are chances for errors. Ugh. I return Jack's stare and then glance around the room. All these people—my friends— would do anything for me. I can't let them get hurt. I have to do something. I look behind me and watch Lilly for a minute. My heart sinks. If not for me, I have to do it for that innocent little girl. My decision's made. "I'll do it." I look each of them in the eye. "I'll meet with him and see what happens. He might very well just want to talk, right?"

"No!" Belle yells.

"Baby, you don't have to. We'll find another way." Jack pleads, pulling me close. He tucks my head under his chin, wrapping his arms around me. I let him this time.

"I need to." I whisper. "This needs to end."

CHAPTER TWENTY – FIVE
Jack

Her decision's made. She won't change it, I know. Of what I have learned about my woman is that she's stubborn. We'll have to make do with what she has decided and protect her in any way possible. I kiss the top of her head and release her. She and Belle move to the couch to watch over Lilly. I sit in a chair at the table and pick up her phone. Since we are doing this, we are doing it right.

Where and when?

I type in a message and send. I look to Dex who sits behind his laptop. "See if you can get a trace. A location, anything." He nods and starts typing. "Do you think any of your men would come help out on this job?" I ask.

"I have a few, yeah. We'll keep her safe, Jack. We got this, man." He says as his fingers fly across the keyboard at quick speeds.

Friday. Don River Bridge. 6pm. Alone.

An abandoned bridge area. What the fuck is the man up to? I don't trust him. I don't think he wants to just talk, that's for sure. I crack my neck to relieve some tension and type back.

I'll be there.

I put the phone down and look over at Dex who's still busy typing away. "Anything?"

He looks up and grimaces. "It's a burner phone, which we figured. It's bouncing off of several towers in the area. So we know he's close, but I can't pinpoint his location. He is for sure in the area though."

I nod my head in understanding. I remember when we were searching for Mike, the bastard that was hunting down Belle. He too used a burner phone. I wish our technology could bust through those stupid things.

"Thanks, man. He wants to meet Friday. So, if you can get some men here for then, that'd be great." I begin to plan what needs to be done. I won't let anything happen to Mel.

He grins at me. "Not a problem. I'm on it."

I get up and head to the kitchen. I'm in need of caffeine and the one cup I had before coming here this morning just isn't cutting it. I see that Gabe has a pot ready, so I get a mug from the cupboard and pour a cup. I scoop a teaspoon of sugar in it, stir, and take a sip. Perfect. Leaning against the counter I think back to a few months ago, when we were in almost a similar situation. Well, not similar, but dangerous. Mike, Belle's past came knocking. Shit hit the fan then and Belle got hurt. I pray to God that we don't have the same outcome in this scenario. Sipping my coffee, I hear footsteps. In walks Mel. Her slender body's covered in tight fitting blue jeans and a purple slim fitting tee shirt today. I can make out every curve of her beautiful body from her rounded hips, to her perky tits. I mentally groan and smile to her. Every day I crave her more. A look, a touch, everything about her is my undoing and I love it. She's my mate for life and I'm never letting her go.

"Hey. Is there more of that?"

I set my mug down and reach for another. I fill it up and hand it to her. She opens the fridge to grab some cream and pours some in. "Sugar?" Raising her eyebrows, she sticks her cup out. I scoop a spoon full into her cup and stir. "Thank you." She takes a sip and purrs. "Perfect." Moving towards me, she sets her mug on the counter and presses her body against mine. Reaching her arms up, she wraps her arms around my neck. She rests her chin on my chest, looking up at me. "I love you, you know." She whispers.

I wrap my arms around her and look into her glistening eyes. "I love you, too." Leaning down I press my lips to her warm, pink ones. Leaning my forehead against hers, we just stare at each other. We take this moment to be together, to be just us—a couple without all the drama and danger. I can see the love in her eyes, the depth of her feelings go far, as do mine. I can't believe it took me all these years to find this feeling. It's the best feeling in the world. I'm happy—even if she was teasing me this morning. I raise my lips into a smirk, "So, my little tease."

She fakes being shocked. "Me? A tease?" She laughs. "Okay, maybe a little."

"You owe me for this morning. My shower was awfully cold because of that little show you gave me."

She blinks a few times, smiling, licking her lips, acting innocent. "Show? I was just showing you what was yours." She bites her bottom lip.

153

I move a hand down to her bottom and smack her ass just hard enough to leave a little sting. She flinches. "Yes, it's mine. It's gorgeous and will never be shared with anyone." I rub the spot I just smacked.

"Agreed."

"Good girl."

She pulls away and picks up her coffee. "Do you think later we can go pick up some iced coffee? This will do for now, but I'd love an iced coffee." She takes a sip and leans against the counter, mimicking me.

"I'm sure that can be arranged. For now, we need to get things set up for your meeting. Today's Tuesday, the meeting is Friday. We have lots to do still."

She blows out a breath. "I know. I just wish it was over already. Any word about Matt and Riley?"

Well, shit. We have been so focused on her father, we haven't checked in on our leads dealing with those bastards. "I will ask around today." We both head back out to the living room.

"I need to head down to the bar." Gabe looks to the clock. "I told my manager that I'd open today. Are you guys okay here?" Gabe asks as he shoves his wallet in his pocket and picks up his cell from the table.

"Yeah, no problem, man. Go ahead. We'll text if we need you." I tell him as he heads for the door.

"Thanks. I'm just down stairs if anything happens." He nods and heads out.

It's just the five of us and Lilly left. We haven't had lunch and no one has mentioned food. I'm starving. With my cell, I dial and order a couple pizzas for delivery. Half hour. I'll fill my gut with greasy pizza in half an hour. Good. I look over at Lilly and wonder about the things she may have witnessed with having the senator in her life. I don't want to pull her into this, but I don't want her traumatized either. "Hey, Sebastian, can we talk?" I ask, insinuating that this talk will be private.

He switches seats to be closer and leans on his elbow on the table. "Sure, what's up?"

I glance quickly over at the beautiful little blonde girl to make sure she isn't listening before I start. "Has the senator ever had contact with your little girl?" I speak low, hoping my voice doesn't travel.

Sebastian looks to his little girl and smiles. "Yeah, she has, but nothing but positive dealings, and in short periods." He turns his attention back to me. "I have a neighbor back home that I basically adopted as a nanny. I told her I had a boss that I didn't trust around my daughter and she understood. She protects Lilly like her own. If I ever had to leave in the middle of the night, Silva was there. No questions. Silva's like a sister to be honest. The senator doesn't know about her. He thinks I just brought Lilly to day care. I'm very careful when it comes to her."

I blow out a breath, thankful that the little girl has nothing to fear at this point. I hope once we take the senator down, all our fears of harm to Mel and Lilly go away and never return.

"That's good. You're a great father, man." I pat him on the back and sit back.

"Thanks. I do try."

Matt

I listen as Mick drones on and on about needing another girl for the next shipment. Since Riley and I fucked up with our last girl a few weeks ago, Mel, our revenge chick, Mick has been crueler than usual to us. Mick gave us specs on the type of woman he wanted and Mel fit perfectly. It wasn't the plan Riley and I had for her, but hell if we have a little fun and make some money off of her, why not? But like I said, we fucked up.

Now we are out searching for another girl that looks like her to sell so Mick doesn't cut our balls off. We are sitting in the van in the Tim's parking lot where I see a girl who looks perfect. "What about her?" I ask Riley.

He looks, narrowing his eyes. "Nope, too short. Let's find another parking spot." Riley tells me, so I pull out of the spot and start driving.

We are driving by the bar that Mike told us about when I see a woman that looks just like Mel. I grind my teeth. It's not possible. She's dead. "Is that Mel?" I ask Riley as I point toward the dark-haired beauty heading in a door by the bar.

He looks over and curses. "Shit. Yes. She survived." He grinds out. "Pull over somewhere close. I want to finish what we started with her."

I pull the van up ahead and wait. "We'll wait and follow her for when she is alone. Strick when the time is right."

"Fucking right we will."

CIRCUMSTANCES UNRAVELED

CHAPTER TWENTY – SIX
Mel

It's Wednesday. Belle works today. Dex stays with Sebastian and Lilly at my place as extra protection. Jack left his truck here for me today so I'm able to get around if I want. He asks Gabe to go investigate the area I'm to meet with my father on Friday.

Since Jack left this morning, I've had this eerie feeling. Someone's watching me. Goosebumps cover my flesh and the little hairs on my neck stand up. I move the window by the couch and look out. I see nothing. The sun is shining, birds are singing. I see no shadows of people and no movement of anything other than the branches from the trees blowing in the slight breeze. I know the windows and doors are locked. Jack double checked them before he left. Maybe I'm just being paranoid.

I head to the bedroom to put some clothes on. I can't wear just Jack's tee shirt alone. I open my bag of clothing and pull out some clean ones.

After I dress I put my sneakers on, grab my purse, toss my phone in it, pick up the keys to the truck, and unlock the front door. Blowing out a breath, I open the door slowly. No one's there. Phew. I step out, turning to lock the door. Once locked, I take in the scenery. Still there's nothing out of the ordinary. I walk to the truck, unlock it, and hop in—immediately locking it with me inside. "Calm down, Mel. You're starting to lose it." I say out loud to myself.

I start the truck, look around, and put it in reverse. Backing up I notice a van sitting at the end of the driveway. A chill runs down my spine again. What the fuck? Pulling out on the road, I'm side by side with the van so I look in. FUCK! It's them. Matt and Riley. I throw the truck in drive and push the pedal to the floor. How'd they find me? They left me for dead! How do they even know I'm alive? I need to get to Jack.

I don't know the area very well where Jack moved. I only know how to get to Gabe's. With my panic on a rise, I reach for my purse, digging in it, I pull out my phone. I know using your phone and driving is wrong, but fuck it. This is an emergency.

I glance in my mirror. The van is tailing my every move. My heart starts to race. I push my foot harder on the pedal. Quickly I dial Jack. It rings. And rings.

"Pick up, Jack. Come on. Pick up." My voice starts to rise. Adrenaline increases with the rush of my heart.

Fourth ring and Jack answers. "Hey, baby. What's up?" He answers as if there's nothing wrong. Well fuck that, everything's wrong!

"Matt! Riley! Van! Chasing me." All of the words I give are short. I blurt them out because it gets hard to breathe. My panic begins to overpower me.

I hear rustling over the phone. "Slow down, Mel. What's going on? I heard something about Matt and Riley."

"They fucking found me and are chasing me in your truck!" I yell as clear as I can. I weave around another car, braking before I slam into a car that decides that it's going to turn. I ignore my blinker and whip the truck around the corner. "Help, Jack. Where do I go?" Tears start to fall down my face.

"Meet us at the police station."

I don't let him finish. There are several stations in the city. "Which fucking one?" I look in the mirror. The van is still on my ass, so close it could hit me.

"Fuck, baby. Try and calm down. The one closest to your work. Try not getting into an accident on the way. Love you."

I throw the phone aside and put both hands back on the wheel. I'm pretty sure I know how to get to that station. I haven't really been paying attention to street signs since I left Jack's in a hurry, but I'll do my best.

I look up and read the sign. Okay, I know this street, I got this. I brake, slowing down for the traffic. Looking both ways and seeing no cars, I stomp on the pedal and squeal the tires, speeding through the light and driving toward my destination. I think maybe if I lose them it'd be a good idea, but then I think not. If I'm going to the police, I can trap them. I look in the mirror to see they're still there and they are.

I take a breath and try to calm myself. I know what my plan is. I need to slow my panic attack down. I take a right just before the light changes. The van runs the light, just as I thought it would. Weaving in and out of cars, I know I'm not far now. I take a left knowing that the station is just up on the left and slow my speed. I watch in my mirror that the van is still there, which it is. I stop in front of the station and just sit in the truck. The van pulls up behind me and no one gets out.

Jack said to meet him here. Where the fuck are they? I look around and I see movement. Matt and Riley must see them too because the van starts to move. It pulls around, the passenger window is down and a gun is pointed my way. I duck just as a shot is fired. My window blasts apart just as three more shots are fired. Glass sprays across my torso, I cover my face as it flies around me. I hear a crash and look up in time to see the van crash into a vehicle at the stop light. Jack and two police officers stand at the side of the road with guns raised, pointing at the van.

Jack lowers his gun, puts it back in the back of his jeans and rushes over to me. Cracking the door open, he reaches in and pulls me out, setting me on my feet beside the truck. He starts wiping the shards of glass off my body and looking me over for injury. "Are you hurt?"

I look myself over, breathing erratically, trying to calm down. "I don't think so." I look back at his truck and wince. "Your truck."

He touches my forehead in a wiping motion and it stings a little. "Fuck my truck, you're hurt. You're bleeding." He wipes the blood on his jeans and swipes his thumb over the cut on my forehead again. "Let's get you inside and cleaned up."

I nod and look over at the van. "What about Matt and Riley?"

Jack shakes his head. "Not your problem anymore. Let the police handle them."

I watch as more police officers come rushing out of the building (armed) and surround the van. Jack escorts me into the station where Gabe waits with a phone to his ear. "She's safe. I'll call you later, babe." He hangs up the phone. "That was Belle, she was worried."

"Thanks." I tell him as I sit down in the chair Jack offers me. A lady, the secretary I assume, comes to the door and hands him a first aid kit. Jack takes it and kneels in front of me.

"Let's get you fixed up."

CIRCUMSTANCES UNRAVELED

CHAPTER TWENTY – SEVEN
Jack

When I see that van pull out, I yell for the officers to get outside as quickly as they can and I run. I pull my gun from the waist of my jeans, remove the safety, and aim right for the bastard driving. Mel looks my way, a distraction. I don't see the window go down on the passenger side and then a gun stick out. When I do, I take my shot, but not before the passenger takes his. I pray to God that Mel ducks in time. I hear two other shots fire from behind me, then I watch the suspects van crash into a vehicle at the stop light right ahead. I'm not thinking about those men anymore. My thoughts are on my woman. Mel. I put the safety back on and shove my gun back into my pants. Running to her, making sure she's safe, is my priority.

I get Mel all fixed up. A few scratches and a large cut on her arm from the shattered glass is all she suffered from on the surface. I know her anxiety's probably through the roof. Gabe calls for a guy to come get my truck, to put a new driver's side window in. We're told it'll only be a few hours.

A Detective Johnson joins us in the room. He wants to talk to Mel about Matt and Riley. Apparently the case has been handed over to him since he works closely with the government agency. I try to direct him to Dex—which he's okay with doing—but he still needs to talk to Mel. He says he just has a few questions, that he'll be quick. So I let him ask them.

He sits at the table across from Mel with a note pad and pencil. "Mel…I know this is hard, but can you tell us who Matt Booker and Riley Daniels were working for or with?" He asks in a soothing, curious voice.

She licks her dry lips and swallows. "I don't know who they worked for, but there was a third guy. I don't know his last name, but he went by the name Mick. He has an accent. Spanish, I think. He's older than the other two." She starts to pick at her fingers.

Detective Johnson writes the information down and looks back at her. "Thank you, Mel. The man you know as Mick, is Mickell Sonar. He's pretty popular in the sex trafficking ring. He's known to us."

Mel bites her lip. "So, you have Matt and Riley in custody?"

Detective Johnson looks to me, questioning with his eyes. I nod. "Mr. Booker and Mr. Daniels are deceased. You don't have to worry about them anymore. We'll deal with Mr. Sonar, you shouldn't fear him. Once he realizes his scum of men are gone, he won't try going for you. We know how he works."

A tear runs down her cheek, I reach over to wipe it away. "Well, that's something. Thank you, Detective Johnson."

"No, thank you." He stands, putting his note pad in his pocket, he nods to Gabe and I and leaves the room.

"Well, that's one problem out of the way." Gabe mutters as he leans against the window sill, typing on his phone, probably updating Sebastian.

"Sebastian?" I ask him, nodding toward his phone.

"Nah, man. I have Dex going to your place, setting up some camera's just in case." He looks at Mel and I. "Just because Matt and Riley are out of the way, doesn't mean her father won't do something." He looks back down to his phone.

Smart man, my friend is. I chuckle to myself. "Good idea, man."

"I need a drink, Jack." Mel says, softly. Looking up at me from her chair, steri-strips on her forehead from the cut she got from the glass, she's still beautiful. I can't deny her.

"What would you like, baby?"

She bites her cheek while she tries to decide. I smile at the cute gesture, "A pop of some kind, please. Whatever you can find is fine." She blinks her bright eyes at me and like I said, I can't deny her.

"Be right back." I wink at her and leave in search of the pop machine.

I wander the hallway until I find the machine. Pulling change from my pocket, I slip some in the machine and choose Root beer. I grab the cold drink and head back to my woman. It'd figure, just when we think we're getting our shit under control, those stupid asses had to show face. I'm just glad they were stupid enough to follow Mel to the police station. Now, they're out of the way, it's time to deal with senator

167

Waters. How he managed to stay on the senate for so long doing all the shit he has, I'll never know. But it's time he comes crumbling down and pays for his sins.

Back in the room, I hand Mel her drink. I look to Gabe and ask. "How much longer 'til my truck is back?"

"I will text now and see." He responds.

"Thanks."

I kneel in front of Mel and set my hands on her knees. "How are you doing? Has my firecracker settled down?" I grin as I run my thumb back and forth over her knee.

She sets her drink on the table and places her hands on top of mine. "Yes, Jack. Your firecracker has simmered down. My nerves have settled and I'm actually pretty tired. Car chases take a lot out of you, eh?"

I laugh a little and shake my head. I pull my hands out from under hers and pat them. "Only you, baby, only you." Standing up I look to Gabe with raised eyebrows. "Well?"

He shoves his phone in his pocket and walks toward me. "They'll be here in ten minutes, man. I'm going to head home. If you need me, you know how to contact me." He pats my back and heads out.

I watch him leave and nod. "Home sounds good. What do you think?" I lay my hand before me, inviting Mel to take it. Helping her up from the chair, I pull her close, breathe her in, and smile. Mine. "Let's go outside and wait."

CHAPTER TWENTY – EIGHT
Mel

Now that my adrenaline subsides, exhaustion takes over. I can't wait to shower and crash. Sleep hasn't been fruitful these past few days. I had one great night of sleep, but the others? Not so much. My anxiety has my mind running marathons and then comes the nightmares…I want to tell Jack, but he has enough on his plate.

It's still early afternoon. A little nap will do wonders for me. I'm sure sleep and some Jack time will pull me from this slumber and everything will be right in my world again. Oh, wait. No, it won't. I still have to deal with my father in a few days. Fuck. I tuck myself closer to Jack as we stand on the side walk, wrapping my arms around him.

"You okay, Mel?" He asks. His voice is full of concern.

I yawn, covering my mouth, slightly embarrassed. "Yes, just tired is all."

He wraps his arm around my shoulder and starts to rub it up and down. It's relaxing. "We'll be home soon and you can rest. Just a few more minutes."

He finishes his sentence just as his truck pulls up to the curb. The driver's door opens. A young man gets out and walks over. He hands Jack the keys and nods.

"Here you go, Jack. Gabe says the bill's all taken care of."

Jack and I both look to the young man a little shocked (but thankful) as he walks toward another truck that pulled up behind Jack's. He hops in and that truck drives off.

"Looks like I owe Gabe a favor now." Jack chuckles as he moves to open the passenger side door. I move to get in, noticing that all the broken glass is gone, the front seat area has been wiped clean, and a new air freshener is hanging from the rear-view mirror. I smile.

I flick the lemon scented freshener and laugh. "I think the repair man is trying to tell you something." The door shuts, but I hear Jack laugh before it closes completely. He rushes around the front of the truck, opens his door, and hops in.

"My truck didn't smell before, baby. You're just trying to rile me up." He smirks and shakes his head. "Don't get me going if you want to nap when we get home."

I bite my lip and look out the windshield. I stay quiet because I know if I don't shut up I'll be in trouble. I'm tired. I want to nap. After some sleep, I'm game for some fun.

I stay quiet for the whole drive. Leaning my head against the back of the seat, I fight to keep my eyes open. We pull into the driveway and he puts the truck in park. Jack gets out and looks around before he comes to my door. Why I waited I'm not sure, but he seems happy that I did.

JEAN KELSO

Opening my door, he looks at me with bright eyes and open arms. I reach out for him and he helps me out of the truck. When my feet hit the ground, I wrap my hand in his. He closes the truck door and we head inside hand in hand.

I kick my shoes off by pushing them off at the heels. Leaving them at the door, I head for the comfy couch. "I'll just lie here for a little bit." I curl my arms under the throw pillow on the end of the cushion. It's not long until I'm asleep.

I wake to soft music playing, the lights are dim and something smells amazing. I sit up on the couch and look around. Jack's at the stove and the table's set for two. By George, is Jack being romantic? I think he might be. I grin internally as I stand up and move toward him.

I'm soft with my steps, quiet with my movements. I don't want to startle him, but sneaking up on him is fun sometimes. I move to press my body up against his back—his hard muscular body. I slide my hands up his black tee shirt and hear him groan.

"Oh, baby—we don't have time for dessert first, dinner's ready." He swiftly turns his body around, shocking me with his quick movements. He dips his head down and gives me the pleasure of his warm lips pressed to mine. "Go sit down. I'll bring the food over." He tells me.

I do as I'm told and sit at one of the place settings. "What's for dinner?"

He heads toward the table, carrying a big, glass dish full of something delicious. I can tell by the smell on its own. "Chicken fettucine. Homemade." He sets the dish on the table and returns to the kitchen to grab a serving spoon.

"It smells wonderful." I lean toward the dish, taking a long, slow sniff of the pasta. Damn, does it ever smell good! I lift my plate. "Can you please put some on my plate? I can't wait to try your cooking." I wink at him.

He scoops up a hefty portion and pours it on my plate. "There you go. Enjoy." He then plates some for himself and sits down.

I take a bite and literally moan. Fuck, it's delicious. "Damn, Jack. This is the best chicken fettucine I've ever had." I take another bite and moan again.

Jack stares at me, his eyes glisten as his mouth goes rigid. He licks his lips and shakes his head. "Fuck, baby, you make me horny just by eating. Stop moaning, will ya?" He scoops a mouthful on his fork and eats it.

I giggle and take another bite. I force myself not to moan this time. It's hard not to, the food's so good. "Sorry, baby. But the food's so good. I like what I like and I have to show my appreciation." Taking a sip of the water that was set with my place setting, I watch him for his reaction.

"You can show me your appreciation after dinner." He winks and takes another bite of his food.

I finish my noodles, wipe my face with a napkin, and stand up with my empty plate. I head to the kitchen and set my dishes on the counter. "Thank you for cooking dinner. Would you mind if I go shower?" I ask as I walk over to him, leaning down and wrapping my arms around his neck and placing my head on his shoulder. Looking into his eyes, I see that mischief reflects back at me. I don't know what plans he has for me, but after today's events I need to wash the filth of Matt and Riley from my mind. The thought that they were anywhere near me again makes me feel like I bathed in dirt. I need to scrub my skin and wash away the day.

"You go ahead and get showered. I'll clean this up." Jack tells me as he stands from the table, turning in my arms and pressing his lips to mine in a sweet, tender kiss.

CIRCUMSTANCES UNRAVELED

CHAPTER TWENTY - NINE
Jack

Mel goes to shower and I clean up the dishes. I imagine today has been very stressful for her. She needs some alone time, some peace and quiet. I'll give her everything she needs, everything she deserves.

I head to the bedroom and pick up the mess I left there when I showered. I managed to sneak one in while Mel slept, in between meal prep and cooking. Fixing up the bed, I notice that I left my gun out on my dresser. I don't need that reminder out in the open for Mel to dwell on, so I take it from my dresser and put in the top drawer.

Looking in the mirror, I see a tired man. Stress wears a man down. I have so many things to be thankful for and Mel's number one. I suppose being alive should be first, but having a woman to love makes it all worth it.

I look around the room and I smile to myself. Nodding, I feel proud. This is my house. I've finally put down roots. It feels good. I think I'll be putting a leave in at the FBI and doing most of my work at CSIS. I want to stay close to home.

Hearing the water turn off, I begin to rid myself of my shirt. I pull it up and over my head, tossing it into my laundry hamper. I pull my socks off, one by one and in the hamper, they go. I lean against my dresser and wait.

Mel walks in with a towel wrapped around her naked, wet body unaware of me watching her. She walks over to the bed where her bag sits on the floor.

"Hey there, firecracker," I say with as much sex in my voice as I can.

Mel jumps and drops her towel. "What the…?" She yells moderately as she turns around to find me smirking at her.

I stare at her now naked body. My eyes drift up and down. I whistle at her beauty. "Perfect. Just amazing." I tell her.

"You scared the shit out of me, Jack." She bends down to grab the towel, but I'm quicker. I rush over and grab the towel first.

"No need to cover up, baby. Let me look at you." I set the towel on the bed, take her hands, and raise them up so I can look her over. I lick my lips and swallow. I spin her in a slow circle and groan. My cock gets harder by the minute. "Never hide this body from me. You're beautiful." I pull her close and wrap my arms around her. I imagine she can feel my cock press against her, but tonight's not about me. I want it to be for her.

All for her.

I pull back and place a light kiss on her lips. "Lay on the bed, baby."

Mel does as I ask and I smile. I walk around the bed until I get to the end. I crawl up onto it and kneel there, just watching her breathe, her chest moving up and down, her gorgeous breasts begging to be touched. I move up her body—slowly—lightly touching her, sweeping my fingers along her skin, enticing goose bumps to rise on her flesh. I kiss her inner thighs, blow on her warm pussy, teasing as I move up her stomach, nipping, licking and kissing until I get my mouth on a breast. I suck a nipple into my mouth and I hear Mel moan. I roll her other nipple with my fingers until it's taut. Releasing her breast with a pop, I switch to the other, moving my tongue around the nipple and sucking it in. She moans again. Her skin's so soft and sensitive. I look up to her face and watch her reactions. She's breathing erratically and biting her lip.

I bite lightly on her nipple, lick it, and move down her stomach, tracing with my fingers as I go. At the top of her pussy, I lightly blow on her skin. She arches her back, begging for me to take what I want.

I plan to.

I caress my fingers across her hips, down her thigh and into her warmth. I feel her shiver to my touch. I swipe my finger up and down a few times in her wet slit before I sink my middle and ring finger inside.

"Jack…" She moans loudly as she lifts her hips to meet my hand.

Her sweet smell begins to drive me wild. I thrust my fingers in again and again. I can't hold back and delve into her. I lick her glistening pussy and she tastes heavenly. I find her swollen clit with my tongue and flick it once, twice. Mel starts to buck her hips, moaning my name. I know she's getting close.

I thrust my fingers harder, faster. I gently bite her clit and lick around it. Her body tenses as her breathing becomes rapid.

"That's it, baby, come for me."

Mel lets go, screaming my name. "Jack…Yes!" I continue fingering her and licking her pussy as she comes. I pull my fingers out, sucking them clean, and wipe my mouth with the back my hand.

I crawl up her body and slam my mouth to hers. I take the kiss deep, battling my tongue with hers. I nip her bottom lip, kiss her chin and down her neck. I move to my side and roll her to spoon with me.

Her whole body feels lax, sated. I wrap my arms around her and cuddle her. My cock is rock stiff, but like I said, it's not about me tonight. I'm not selfish. Well, maybe I am, but only for Mel.

"Jack? What about you? I can feel you poking me." She tries to turn over, but I don't let her. I pull the blankets up and over us.

"I'm good, baby. Tonight was for you. Just relax and get some sleep now. I love you." I press a kiss to her shoulder and blow out a breath. I love this woman so much. I'm not looking forward to Friday.

She entangles her arms and legs with mine and sighs. "I love you too, Jack."

CHAPTER THIRTY
Mel

It's Friday. Today's the day. The past couple of days have been hectic. The men have been planning everything, crossing the 'T's' and doting the 'I's' for what's supposed to go down tonight. I have yet to make up to Jack the orgasm he gave me the other night, but in time (if I survive) I'll double it for him. It's the least I can do.

It's only five in the morning. Jack's still sleeping. He looks so handsome lying in bed with the sheet barely covering his masculine body. I love his body. I love all of him. My sexy savior.

I couldn't sleep last night because of all the thoughts going through my head about the upcoming danger. I don't want anyone getting hurt.

I came to a conclusion a few hours ago. I'm doing this on my own. My father's my problem. I need to deal with him on my own. I watched where Jack put his gun last night, so while he sleeps, I'm going to sneak it and take it with me for my protection.

I know I'm stupid to go alone on this, but it has to be me. I've been running scared my whole life and it's time to stop it. I need to face my demon head on.

I manage to dress without waking Jack. His gun's in my bag along with my cell phone. I grab my jacket and quietly head out the door, careful not to shut it loudly.

I've been walking for about a half hour and haven't received any texts. Feeling like I'm in the clear, I pull out my phone and pull up my texts. I find the one from my father and start typing.

Let's meet earlier. Say an hour?

I check my surroundings making sure no cars are coming and I cross the street.

My phone beeps so I look.

Eager to see me, daughter?

I huff out a breath.

Cut the shit. Can we meet, or not?

I can just imagine what he is thinking. I never once swore at him in my early ages. I'm feeling brave at the moment. I don't know how long I'll feel this way, but I plan to use it for as long as I can.

I'll see you soon.

I close out the text messages and pull up taxi services. I dial the first one and give my location by the street names I'm currently at.

The taxi drops me off at my destination, the Don River Bridge, a half hour later. Stupid city traffic makes the trip longer than it should, but it gives me time to pull my strength together, to get my mind set on what's going to happen.

The bridge is abandoned and sort of scary looking. I grip my purse tight and start walking around. It's shortly after six thirty in the morning, the sun begins to shine, but the warmth it provides doesn't help uphold the bravado I carry.

The area is huge, old and, dilapidated. The bridge is broken in several areas, condemned with rat's nests in its dark corners. I can just imagine why my father wanted to meet here.

I see no sign of my dear old dad yet, so I find a bench to sit on and wait. He said he'd be here, so I know he won't be long.

Seagulls fly overhead in search of their next meal. Creaking noises make me tense and grip my purse tighter in my lap. I look around, watching for movement.

A shadow approaches from the east out of nowhere and I feel like my body jumps out of its skin, but I hold myself still. I watch as my father walks toward me, a black trench coat covers his large body, grey hair covers his head. His eyes mirror my own.

"Hello, Sydney. Or should I say, Mel?" He says with a terse voice.

I stand from the bench. Pushing my shoulders back, I look him in the eye. "Father."

He holds his hands out showing they are empty. Raising his eyebrows, he asks. "No, 'I've missed you? It's nice to see you?' Anything?"

You've got to be kidding me. This man standing before me thinks he deserves such gestures from me? "No, sorry. Not today. What do you want?"

He steps toward me and the hair on my neck stands up. I can't let him get too close.

"Your mother. What do you think you saw?" He takes another step.

I step back, slowly easing my hand into my purse. "You know what I saw." I spit out. My anger rises to the surface.

He watches me move my hand and narrows his eyes. "Don't be stupid, girl." He growls as he reaches inside his coat.

I pull out the gun, wrap my hand around it properly, and place my finger on the trigger—pointing it at my father.

My father's quick and mirrors my actions. A gun points at me in return.

"I think we have a problem, Dad" I grunt.

CHAPTER THIRTY - ONE
Jack

I stretch in bed and yawn as I roll over to wrap my arms around my love. She's not there. I open my eyes and blink. "Mel?" I call out and get no answer.

I kick the blankets off and get out of bed. I check the time. It's only six in the morning. I don't hear the water running, so I pull on the jeans I left beside the bed the night before. I grab a clean t-shirt and pull it over my head. I leave the bedroom in search of my woman. Room to room I go and she's nowhere to be found. Her purse is gone. Her phone, too.

Today's the day we confront her father, but she wouldn't do anything stupid...would she? I check to see if she left me a note, but there's nothing. I get a sinking feeling in my gut and check for my gun. Opening the drawer, my gut sinks to the floor. "Fuck." I yell out.

I head back to the living room in search of my phone. I need Gabe, Sebastian, and Dex in on this. I need to save my woman before it's too late. I can't believe she would risk her life like this. Who knows what the senator will do to her once he gets his hands on her?

Immediately I dial Gabe. He picks up on the first ring. "It better be an emergency. It's barely morning, man." He growls in a groggy voice.

"Mel's gone. She took my gun and is gone, man." I run my fingers through my hair and pace my living room floor. I look outside and see my truck's still there. Thank fuck for that, but that makes me wonder how she's getting around. And when the fuck did she leave? Fuck, fuck, fuck. I shove my feet into my shoes, grab my keys from the counter and head out the door.

"Okay, calm down, Jack. We'll find her. You think she went to meet him?" I hear him wrestling around, probably getting dressed. I hear Belle mumbling in the background.

I open my truck door and hop in, starting the engine. "Where else would she go? I'm going to call Dex and have him track her phone while I head that way. Meet you there."

"Gotcha."

We hang up and I dial Dex. "Morning, Jack. Why are you calling so early?" Dex is a morning person, but still I didn't expect such a pleasant greeting.

"Hey, Dex. I need you to track Mel's phone. She has my gun and she's missing." I rush my words as I start driving down the street.

"Shit. Seriously? I'm on it. Call you back in a few." He tells me and hangs up.

I cut some corners and weave in and out of traffic. Rush hour sucks in the morning, everyone trying to get to work on time.

My phone rings, I answer to Gabe shouting words. "I called Sebastian. He's heading to the police station with the files. I'm on my way to the bridge. I'll meet you there. Stay safe, man."

"You, too." I tell him and hang up. Things are moving fast, but my stubborn woman had to go rogue and make shit fly. We have no choice now. I just hope we get to her before anything happens.

Looking over my shoulder, checking blind spots, checking mirrors, I maneuver my truck through traffic. I'm not moving as fast as I hoped, but I'm doing the best as I can. I'm on city streets, not the highway so I can't just hop the curb and drive the emergency lane like I would.

My phone rings again. I answer, it's Dex. "She's at the bridge. I'm on my way there now. I pinged the burner phone and it's at the bridge too, Jack. We need to hurry."

"Fuck!" I yell and throw my phone on the dash. I pray as I drive in traffic and around other vehicles. I finally find an open lane and put my foot to the pedal. I speed as fast as I can to get to the bridge.

I pull into a parking lot just down from the abandoned place just as Gabe does. We get out of our vehicles just as Sebastian and a couple police cruisers pull in. Belle comes up to me, eyes watering, fidgeting. "Where is she?"

Gabe wraps his arm around her and directs her back to his truck. "Stay in the truck, babe. We'll get her. You stay put. Stay safe." He kisses her on the lips and comes back over.

I notice Lilly isn't with Sebastian. She must be at the station. Thank fuck, that's one thing I don't need to worry about. Sebastian and a couple of officer's head in our direction.

"Hey." I nod to Sebastian. "How are things on your end?" I ask him, knowing that he brought all the files to the station before he came here.

"I was on the phone with one of Dex's connection's most of the night, and the files are at the station for CSIS to pick up." He looks to the officers with him and nods. "These guys here are hopefully going to take custody of Douglas and then it's out of our hands." He rubs his hands together as if he's anxious to get things done.

"Sounds fucking good to me." I tell him and we gather together to strategize a plan of attack.

CHAPTER THIRTY - TWO
Mel

"You won't pull the trigger. You don't have the guts. You're too weak—just like your mother." My father sneers at me.

I hold the gun up still aiming, but my arm starts to shake. I can't let him see my fear, see my weakness. The longer I have a gun pointing at me, the harder it is for me to stay strong.

"You really don't know me anymore, father. You never really did know me." I take a slow deep breath trying to steady myself.

Douglas takes a step closer and I tense, gripping the gun tighter. "I don't need to know who you are to get rid of you. All I need to know is that you're a problem, a problem that I need to solve, so that' what I'm going to do."

I catch a shadow move in my peripheral vision. And then another. My breath catches and my heart rate speeds up. Did my father bring some goons with him? I step back and almost trip. Panic begins to fight what strength I have left. "I've never told the police about you." I mumble quickly, trying to keep him talking, trying to give myself more time just in case the shadows are on my side. I quickly glance to my left, then to my right, the shadows are moving still.

"I don't care that you never told. You're still a pain in my ass that needs taking care of. I should've taken care of you fifteen years ago instead of having Sebastian deal with it. That simpleton chicken shit, he's next on my list." He sneers moving closer as he talks.

Shadows move into the light and relief overcomes me. Jack. Gabe. Police. I step back and stumble, falling to the ground, the gun slipping from my hand gliding a foot out of reach. "No…" I cry.

My father laughs as he stands over me, gun pointing down toward my head. "You lose."

"Stop right fucking there!" I hear Jack yell as he runs toward me with a gun drawn. Gabe comes from another direction with a gun in his hand as well. They both stop just feet away.

"Police. Drop your gun and put your hands in the air." An officer shouts with his gun pointed toward my father. Another officer comes out from behind a bush with his gun pointed in his direction too. Lastly comes Sebastian. He walks toward us with a gun in hand. We're surrounded. My father's surrounded. My chest pounds with relief, but also with fear. I still have a gun pointed at me and it only takes a split second for something to happen.

With his gun still aimed at me, my father looks around at all the weapons and the faces attached to the weaponry.

"Stay back! I'll shoot her." Douglas yells out, flexing his hand around the gun. His jaw ticks with anger and obvious frustration.

188

Jack takes a cautious step forward. Setting his gun on the ground, he raises his hands up. "Let's talk about this.

I watch as everything plays out. My father whips his head around, looking where everyone is—though he appears scared from his lack of options. The gun never leaves where it's pointing…still at me. Jack takes another step in as the hustle and bustle of the surrounding ground works its way a little closer as well.

"I said don't fucking move!" My father screams as he leans down and grabs me by my hair, pulling me up to stand beside him. He points the gun to my head and growls. "Take another step and I'll put a fucking bullet in her head." He looks to Jack as he's in mid step. Jack stops.

With his hands still raised, Jack nods. "Alright, I'm stopping. What do you want? We'll get you whatever you want."

My father grips my hair tighter and I wince. Clenching my eyes tight, I do my best to hold the tears back. I'm not ready to die. I look around at the men, staring each of them in the eye, pleading with them, begging for them to do something. My hearts racing, chest constricting as my breathing turns to gasps for air with fear of the worst outcome.

"Please, Dad. Don't do this." I beg him, reaching my hands up to my hair, to his hand, trying to get him to release his tight hold. "If you ever loved me, you'll end this now."

I feel the barrel of the gun press harder to my skull and I sob. "Love is just a feeling that destroys lives. I hate feelings. I have no feelings. Especially for you." He grits out as he looks me in the eye.

While he's distracted talking to me, the men change positions. This catches my father's eye and immediately turns his attention back to everyone else. "Let me leave with my daughter. This has nothing to do with you." He grunts as he pulls on my hair and tries to start moving forward.

I can feel my hair ripping from my skull. It hurts like hell. I can't stop the tears from falling down my cheeks. I swallow and cry out. "Please, stop this. I beg of you." A gun shot rings in the air and it's like my heart stops. The grip on my hair is gone and my father falls to the ground beside me. Everyone begins to run around, toward me, to my father. I look around, bawling, in shock. My eyes drop to my father's now lifeless body. Blood starts to pool around his head. I look up and search for the man I love.

I find who I'm looking for and run to him. With his arm's open, I hit his body hard and wrap my arms around him, squeezing tight. Safe. I let the tears go. Jack holds me in his arms, tucking me into his body allowing me to be free, to be safe. He's my savior, my angel in this life. Without him, I don't think I would've survived these nightmares I've been through. I owe him my life. I owe him my heart. He's now my everything and always will be. "I'm so sorry I didn't wait for you." I mumble through my tears. "I love you so much." My emotions take over as my adrenaline dwindles.

CIRCUMSTANCES UNRAVELED

CHAPTER THIRTY - THREE
Jack

I did my best to control the situation. If Mel ever figures out that I was the bait for the operation, she may never forgive me—but hell, it was worth it. Douglas Waters is gone. While we discussed our strategy to take him down and bring him into custody, even the officers thought outside the box. What's one life, compared to the many that the man has already destroyed? So instead of getting cuffs on the man, we planned to put him down. If I was getting shot in the process, it was going to be my due diligence. I'd do anything to save Mel, in this lifetime and the next.

Confusing the senator with us surrounding him having too many faces to watch, worked out well. Distraction was the key. I don't think Mel even realized that she played a part and she played it well. With Douglas frustrated and his plan off key, Dex snuck around behind him and when the shot was clear, he took it. One bullet to the head and the senator's gone for good. Thank fuck for that.

I wanted to be the one to kill the fucker, but Dex said it'd be less of a hassle with him doing it since he's an actual agent. With the files to cover his ass and the fact that the senator was putting innocents in danger, Dex said that his badge could explain the situation better than a contract PI shooting a political benefactor.

The officers rush to Douglas, making sure he's down for good. Sebastian stands still, in shock. Gabe starts to check the perimeter in case the senator brought back up. The only thing on my mind is my woman. Mel. I look to her and see her moving my way. I open my arms just in time for her body to crash into mine. I wrap my arms around her and feel her body shake, tremble as she cries. I hold her tight and let her get it all out. She apologizes and tells me she loves me, things I already know, but let her say the words anyway. I rub my hand up and down her back, kiss the top of her head. "You're safe now, baby. Nothing can get my firecracker now." I turn us both and start walking us toward the parking lot.

I look to Dex who's on the phone, probably calling the situation in and getting back up to clean things up. I nod to him to indicate that we're heading out and he nods back.

As soon as Belle sees us walking toward the vehicles, she jumps out of Gabe's truck and runs at us. She grabs Mel from my arms and pulls her in for a hug, tears running down her face. "I'm so glad you're okay. I heard a gunshot and I was so scared." Belle rambles on.

I give them a few minutes, watching the girls who are like sisters hold each other close, crying, weeping from the fear of the possible loss they both just experienced. "I was beyond scared. He had a gun to my head. I'm so stupid for thinking I could've done this on my own."

"Damn right you are. I should spank your beautiful ass for even thinking about doing it." I mumble to myself, but I know she heard me. Mel looks over her shoulder at me and frowns.

"I'm sorry, Jack. I didn't want anyone getting hurt. Especially the people I love." She turns from Belle's hold and walks into my arms. Looking up into my eyes she pleads with tear stricken puppy dog eyes. "Will you forgive me?" She licks her lips and blinks.

I hear a car door shut, Mel jumps in my arms. The noise was loud, so I can only assume it scared her a little. Gabe's back from the bridge. He comes over and wraps his arm over Belle's shoulder. I kiss Mel on the forehead and whisper in her ear. "It was just a car door, baby. Breathe. You're safe now. And yes, I forgive you, but I still think you're going to get a good spanking."

She lifts her head up and looks to me. She smiles although I see with her fear, love, and curiosity of the unknown.

"Can we go home now?" She whispers.

Belle looks to Gabe biting her lip. "Yes, let's get out of here. My nerves are shot. No pun intended." She looks at Mel as we grimace.

Sebastian comes walking up to us. His expression's grim. He nods to us as he heads toward the patrol car where his little girl, Lilly sits waiting. How I never noticed her in the car, I don't know. I thought she was safely sitting at the station. Stupid officers should have left her there, not brought her here. "Hey, Sebastian?" I call out feeling bad that his kid has been here the whole time. No child should have had to hear what just went down. I'll file a complaint later.

He looks back at me. "Yeah, man?"

"Thanks for everything. You're welcome to stick around here if you want. Stay at Mel's place for a while." I look down at my woman, take her all in. After everything that has gone down, I'm not letting her out of my sight for a long time. "She's staying with me for a while, so you're welcome to her place."

"I think I'll take you up on that. I don't feel like going back to Washington right now. Thanks." He kneels down after he opens the car door and pulls Lilly into his arms.

Unmarked government cars start to roll into the parking lot, that's our cue to leave. I help Mel into the truck, just was I watch Gabe and Belle pull out. Sebastian has Lilly in his car and they're just leaving, too. It has been a stressful morning and it's not even eight o'clock yet. I don't know if we're needed for questioning. If so, Dex will give us a call. I help buckle my woman up and walk around the front of my truck. I look toward the crime scene once more and blow out my breath. It's over. Relief lifts from my chest and I smile. I open my door and hop in the truck, buckling myself in. I left my keys in the ignition when we arrived, so I start the truck and put it in reverse. I back out of the spot and stick it in drive.

Traffic is still heavy as shit. I'm beginning to hate city driving. Mel's quiet on her side. I look over and see she has her head leaning on the side window. She stares at nothing in particular with her hands in her lap. I reach over and take a hand in mine and give a little squeeze. "Hey."

She looks over at me with a small smile. "Hey back."

I watch the road and glance over at her. "You alright?"

"I think I will be in time."

I stop at a stop light and turn to her. "That's good. Are you hungry? Want to stop somewhere?"

She shakes her head and leans against the window again. "No, thanks. I just want to go home—back to your place…if that's okay with you?"

The light changes, so I start to drive again. Watching where I'm going, I continue to talk. "That's fine with me. I'll do anything for you, Mel. I'd give you the moon if I could." I glance over and smile.

CIRCUMSTANCES UNRAVELED

CHAPTER THIRTY – FOUR
Mel

I didn't get to see who shot my father, but I'm thankful they did. That man doesn't deserve to live for all that he's done. I can breathe easy now knowing that he isn't out there searching for me. I don't have to wonder if his goons are just around the corner. What started with him now ends with him.

I told Jack I wanted to go home to his place and that's where he took us.

I still feel a bit jumpy. Every loud noise has me looking over my shoulder. Jack and I sit on the couch watching Netflix, relaxing. The past few days have been so nerve racking and stressful. Put that together with my kidnapping (and hospital stay) and you have a very alpha man making sure you don't lift a finger. I'm not fragile, I'm not broken…I'm just out of shape right now. I don't know if I'll ever be myself again, but I know as long as I have Jack I'll feel safe and loved.

We just finished watching the most recent episode of the new Archie show and now I'm going to make Jack suffer through a girlie movie. I need something upbeat and happy to cover the pain I've been suffering. I search the list and find The Heat. A little Sandra and Melissa to brighten the day. I look to Jack to see his reaction when I land on the movie, he just smirks.

"Want popcorn, baby?" He asks as he stands and heads to kitchen.

This man claims my heart for sure. He knows I love popcorn with movies. "Extra butter, please."

I wait for Jack to return with the popcorn and press play on the movie. Not even ten minutes in and we're both laughing.

It's been two days since the shooting. Things are starting to settle down. My nerves are calmer, my muscles are less tense, and I can breathe easier. I went to the CSIS local office yesterday with Dex and Jack to give my statement. Sebastian was there, as well. Dex was right about the case with him being lead in the lead—his badge being the best cover for a rogue operation. With our stories matching and Dex's clean shot, it turned into an open and close case. The file's now being sent to Washington. There are cases that are open that need dealing with, but I'm in the clear. Unfortunately, Sebastian will be needed down there for federal statements, but Dex said he could stay here in Toronto until they need him.

This morning Jack made me breakfast in bed and then made mad passionate love to me. His touch has seared my soul with so much love. I don't think he'll have any chance of escaping my heart, ever. He then ran a nice hot bubble bath for me with candles burning in the bathroom. It was sweet and sincere of him. Romantic— a side I haven't seen from him until now. A side I hope he'll continue using because I love it.

It's evening now. Jack went out a few hours ago, said he had a few errands he had to run. My mind began to wander, so I picked up a book and started reading. I didn't realize I had books with me until I dug around in my bag. Belle must have packed them when I was in hospital. When I was released, I just packed more stuff on top of what was inside the bag already. Anyways, the book, it's by a local author and I just adore her. She brings her characters alive describing them so vividly and the things they do and say. I'm laughing so much, I'm in tears. This Helena chick is an amazing writer. I think I'll recommend them to everyone at work when I return.

I'm so distracted by the book I don't notice the time. I hear a vehicle pull in the drive way, so I look out the window. Jack's home. I hear the truck door slam and jump. I guess my nerves are still a little off kilter. It may take a little longer to get over things than I think. I set my book down and meet Jack at the door.

I open the door just as Jack is reaching for the door knob. "Hey, baby."

He grins at me, eyes sparkling. "Hey, back." He walks in and kisses me on the forehead. "What have you been up to this afternoon?" He goes and sets his laptop bag on the floor by the table.

"Reading about beaver and wood." I smirk at him and then bite my lip waiting for his reaction.

He turns to look at me, scrunching his eyebrows. "Excuse me? Reading about beavers and wood? Since when are you interested in our national animal?"

I laugh out loud, I can't control it. I slap my thigh and shake my head. "Oh, my God. No. No, not that."

He leans against the table and watches me intently. "Well, then—what the hell are you talking about?"

I take a deep breath and stop my laughing. I go and pick up my book from the table in the living room and bring it back to show him. The first thing he notices is the semi naked man on the cover. He raises his eyebrows and smirks. I ignore him and open the book flipping through until I find a spot that will explain what I mean and stick it in front of him. "Read this."

He starts to read the paragraph. His expressions change as he reads. He immediately looks up at me, flabbergasted. "What the hell are you reading, woman?"

I try to take the book from him, but he doesn't give it back. "Hey, I want to read some more." I tell him tugging on the book lightly.

He tugs back and playfully growls. "I'm not done reading." I laugh at him and yank the book from his grasp. "This guy's cock has a nickname." He chuckles then relents. "Fine, you can have it back. What would you like for dinner?" He asks as he turns and heads toward the fridge.

"No cooking tonight, baby. Pizza. I want pizza. And for dessert, I want you."

EPILOGUE
Mel

It's been a month since everything went down. Things are going great. I'm back to work and feeling good. Things with Jack and I have moved fast, but I suppose when you find your one true love you jump in with both feet. I'm moving all my stuff in this weekend. Well, what I need at least to be properly moved in. The rest is going into storage. People will say it's too soon, but for me it's just right.

Sebastian's fast tracking for a Canadian Citizenship for Lilly and himself. I'm subletting my apartment to him for however long he wants to stay. So far he hasn't been needed back in Washington, but knows the time will come. We're here for him to watch Lilly when it does.

Gabe and Belle are back to normal. Belle and I are due for a girl's night very soon. When she told me about her and Gabe's play time, I grew intrigued and have been reading about some things. I might bring the topic up with Jack and see what he thinks. I'm sure he will be game, considering the comments made way back when we first met about control and such—and his reaction to my reading genres lately.

Dex hasn't been around since the case ended, but then again I never met the man until shit hit the fan. He seems like a great guy and I hope to see him again.

There are a few single nurses at work that'd love to get together with a handsome man like him.

I'm just leaving work. I'd told Jack I would pick up dinner on the way home tonight. He's been working overtime on a missing child case and I don't want him waiting hand and foot on me anymore. I stop and get an order of Chinese (some of our favorites so we have leftovers for tomorrow) and head home.

I pull in the driveway to see the lights are very dim in the house. This is unusual. I grab my purse and our dinner and head toward the door. I turn the knob and push. Once inside, I see the reason for low lighting. Candles burn on the counters and the tables. All the actual lights are off. I set my purse on the couch and bring the bag of food over to the table and set it down. "Jack?" I call out.

Jack comes walking down the hall wearing only a pair of blue jeans with rips in them, low on his waist. The button is undone. He's topless and is barefoot. "How's my firecracker?" He grins and mischief shines in his eyes.

I take my thin sweater off and set it on the chair. I start walking toward him. "I'm doing good. You hungry?" I ask him, smiling.

"Starving." He says as he walks toward me.

"I have Chinese for us." I look toward the table and back to him.

"I don't want Chinese, baby." His grin gets bigger if that is even possible.

"Oh?"

"I want dessert. I want you." He reaches me, leaning down, scooping me up over his shoulder. He slaps my ass making me laugh. Our sex life has been nothing but amazing. You'd think with having been raped that I'd be skittish, but Jack has helped erase the touch of those men. He has helped me move forward, forward and onward with a future with the man I love.

I smack his ass in return and then squeeze both cheeks. "So, greedy, baby."

"Only for you."

THE END

ABOUT THE
Author

Jean is just a small town girl looking for a little adventure. With her love of reading and writing she wanted to explore and see what her characters could do for her. Being a nurse, a wife, and mother of two boys, she has her hands full, but takes the time to dream among the pages. She is a true blooded Canadian and hopes to explore parts of the world sometime in the future, but for now, she explores in the books she reads and writes. Being a huge Indie Author fan, she has made several friends online and has met a few at book signings. Hoping to one day meet some fans face to face, she would gladly friend you on Facebook, Goodreads, Twitter and Google+. She also has a website where you can order paperbacks and keep up to date on everything.

She can be found on Facebook: https://www.facebook.com/jean.kelso.14

She can be found on Goodreads: https://www.goodreads.com/author/show/8338589.Jean_Kelso

She can be found on Google+ as Barb Jean Kelso Johnson

Website: http://authorjeankelso.wix.com/authorjeankelso

Twitter: https://twitter.com/JeanKelsoAuthor